sister slam
and the Poetic Motormouth Road Trip

sister slam

and the Poetic Motormouth Road Trip

Linda Oatman High

BLOOMSBURY

With loads of gratitude to:

Deborah Warren, my wonderful, sparkly, and smart agent.
Thanks for finding a good home for Sister Slam.

Victoria Wells Arms, a whiz of an editor and a true book angel.
Thanks for giving Sister a home at Bloomsbury.

Carolyn Magner, a cool and crazy chick with no clue as to what a
great writer she is. Thanks for reading and encouraging.

My family, thanks for putting up with the Sister and the Twig in me.
And a special thank-you to my poet son Zach,
who almost washed his face in the bidet.

BLOOMSBURY

Copyright © 2004 by Linda Oatman High
All rights reserved. No part of this book may be used or reproduced
in any manner whatsoever without written permission from the
publisher except in the case of brief quotations embodied in
critical articles or reviews.
Published by Bloomsbury, New York and London
Distributed to the trade by Holtzbrinck Publishers, LLC
Library of Congress Cataloging-in-Publication Data
available upon request
ISBN 1-58234-948-7
Printed in the U.S.A.
1 3 5 7 9 10 8 6 4 2

Bloomsbury USA Children's Books
175 Fifth Avenue
New York, New York 10010

All papers used by Bloomsbury Publishing are natural, recyclable products
made from wood grown in well-managed forests. The manufacturing processes
conform to the environmental regulations of the country of origin.

For Lola Schaefer:
a spectacular friend, writer, teacher,
critiquer. Thanks for helping bring
Sister to life.

Lesson 1

Never Ignore Spam Because It's Not Always What It Seems

Sister Slam I am.
I don't like spam.
Not the fake pink ham
that comes in cans,
or the electronic moronic
supersonic junk mail
that never fails to sail
through your computer screen
like an intruder seen
only by you.

It was the first of June,
and soon, by the next full moon,
I'd be loony with jubilation:
my graduation celebration
would be happening with my

too-little two-person family
in the House of Crapper.

I swear, by every
blood-red hair on my spike-cut head,
or lightning may strike me dead,
that this is my real name:
Laura Rose Crapper.
My lame-brained name
was my main claim to fame
at Banesville High School,
where I wasn't exactly in
the cool group.
The kids of cool in Banesville School
drove brand-new cars
and lived in fancy mansions,
where I liked to imagine
they had monkey butlers.
These kids lived mostly on Sutler
Boulevard, in the rich mountain part
of town.

Pops and I lived down in the hollow,
just us, in a teeny green
submarine of a mobile home,
and I drove
my mom's old clunker car—

a '69 Firebird—
the funky sick color
of rabbit turds
dried in the sun.

Plus, I was way past chunky.
In fact, I was downright
clown-white fat,
and big hippie chicks
in thick-soled
black combat boots
just didn't fit into
the cool kids' group
at Banesville School.
I was an Outsider,
a Misfit, a Freak.

"You leak pain
all over the place,"
announced Ms. Nace,
who was a space case.
She was the school counselor,
and a total waste of time.

"Whatever," I said,
slumped on her dump
of a lumpy old couch.

"Maybe I'm just a grouch,
or a natural grump."

"Perhaps it's depression,"
said Ms. Nace.
"The hurt shows on
your face, and in
the slow pace
of your walk. You sulk."

I just let her talk.

The House of Crapper
used to be happier,
back before cancer
won the war
in my mom's body.

Mom died when I
was nine, in July.
She was only
thirty-five.

I wasn't fine, never again,
but I was *maybe* okay.

So anyway,
it was just a normal day
of formal blue-suit sky
and baby birds
chirping for worms
on the first of June,
and I was checking
my hotmail account,
deleting, weeding out
seedy stuff and junk,
when an ad from *Creative Teen 'Zine*
caught my eye.
"Come Try," it said
in the subject line.

"Try what?" I muttered,
then clicked the mouse
and read the message.

"It doesn't matter
if you're an amateur
or a pro poet. Nobody knows
until they try it, what a riot
it is to sizzle in competition
in the sport of spoken word.
Sixth Annual Tin Can, New Jersey,
Poetry Slam."

Well, wham-bam, thank you, ma'am,
a poetry slam! This was the spam
that saved my life.
This was serendipity:
a true whippity-do
of a gift
come straight
from techno-heaven.

Ever since I was seven
and saw the poet laureate
of the entire United States,
just like an everyday person,
eating a Hershey bar
in the local 7-Eleven,
I'd been revvin'
my poetic inspiration,
ignited with the sensation
that someday I'd be
a famous poet.

I wanted to light up
the night with the genius
of my rhyme schemes.

Well, don't you know it:
this was my chance

to dance in my underpants
with Peter Pan,
the green-jeaned,
flyin' and rhymin' man.
I'd always wanted to slam.

And so had
my best friend, Twig,
an indie-goth-hippie chick like me,
only Pringle's Chip skinny,
whose parents named her for the limb
of a teeny-weeny tree.

Twig and me,
we were a team,
and it seemed
that most of the poets
on TV were like us:
they tended to cuss sometimes
without even trying,
and they weren't afraid
of crying.
They wore black
and they liked Jack Kerouac
and some were wacked
and needed Prozac.

Poets seemed bohemian:
somewhere in between
what-passed-for-normal
and the lunatic crazies
in the Banesville Home
for the Insane.

Well, right there
on that day of June first,
I decided that the worst
thing that could ever happen
was for me to remain forever
tethered to the House of Crapper.

I'd just get me some magic
and a map, and ZAP . . .
I'd travel this nation
and be a sensation!
Laura Rose Crapper
would be one happy rapper . . .
a jazzer, a beboppin', hip-hoppin'
Beat poet, the Queen of Cool,
don't ya know it!

But I'd be a fool,
and that's no bull,
to keep the name

of Laura Crapper,
which sounds like a slacker
or a toilet.

So I changed my name
right there on the spot,
and wow, was it hot,
so hot it sizzled
and blistered my fingers
like Crisco-fried ham.
My new name was Sister Slam!

But damn, Pops got way hot
under the collar
of his Dollar Store
working-stiff shirt
buttoned all the way up
to his neck. (Heck,
Pops puts up with
shirt suffocation
and the humiliation
of dirt-factory work,
all for the perk
of a three-week
paid vacation.
I don't know why,
but he wears a tie

to make cherry pie
at the Mrs. Smith's
factory on Sixth Street,
where the freakin' heat
makes his face
even geek-redder than ever.)

But I never
saw his face
as beet-red
as that day,
when I said that
I'd changed my name
and that after graduation day
I was going away
to take a place
in the Tin Can
Poetry Slam.

"You're not as big as you
think," he sputtered.
"And you've never
driven farther
than the next town
over. And there's
not a thing
wrong with your name, Laura."

He was disconcerted,
but I asserted
my decision, mister,
fixing my vision of fame
firmly in my brain.

"Sister Slam I am,"
I said,
and did he turn red.
I thought I was dead,
he was that red.
Father Strangles Daughter
with Dollar Store Necktie
would be the headline
in the *Daily Local*
(Loco) *News* of Banesville—
Hicksville—Pennsylvania.

"I don't like green eggs
and ham," I said gently,
hoping to joke
his face less red.

Mom and Pops
(before Mom was dead
and I was fat)
used to read

Dr. Seuss books
to me a lot—*The Cat in the Hat*,
and *Red Fish, Blue Fish*,
and *Green Eggs and Ham*—
and probably
that helped
make me into
Sister Slam.

My parents
rocked me to sleep
by reading heaps
of poetry:
Edna St. Vincent Millay
and William Blake,
Edgar Allan Poe
and Van Fernando,
some guy they used
to know in high school.

Mom and Pops
created this
word-addicted
cool-kid-evicted
fat chick
who wanted to be a

butt-kickin', shit-slingin'
road poet.

Pop's eyes misted,
and I knew
that he was wishing
that Mom were here,
missing her
as much as ever.
It never goes away:
the ache for what
used to be.

"Do what you want,"
Pops said,
shaking his head.
His voice was soft.
"You're eighteen,
and you think
you're an adult.
It's not my fault.
It's not your fault.
Do it. I can't stop you anyway."

Hooray. Whuppity-do.
Wham-bam, thank you, Pops.

Damn, that was easier
than a spray of
fake grease
in a hot, sizzling
frying pan.
Better than butter
in the sun.

I grabbed Pops,
wrapping him
in a hug.

My new name—
my claim to fame
in life after Banesville High—
was Sister Slam.

Sister Slam I am.

You Don't Need a List for a Road Trip

Twig and me,
we were getting ready
to take our show on the road,
in my toad-colored bedroom.

It was the day
after our graduation
celebration, and
we were eating
leftover red velvet
cake with white cream frosting.

"That was awesome,
how your pops
made the cake
and decorated
it with the colors

of Banesville High
and a graduate's cap,"
Twig said, dropping
cake crumbs on my bed.

I nodded.
Pops was
a great baker
of cakes.
That's one thing
I'd miss
when I was away.

"Let's make a
list," I said,
"of everything
we need to do
for the road trip."

"We don't need a list,"
Twig said. "Pack clothes.
Write poems. Eat, sleep,
pee, breathe."

"Okay," I said. "Time to create."

Sprawled across
my sloshy waterbed,
we mulled alone then
in our own heads, thinking about
what we could yank out
and put down on paper.

Vapors of poems,
ghost poems,
floated in our
brains, part of us,
but not yet out of us.

Twig broke
the quiet diet of words.

"Remember what you called
your pillows,
when we were little?"
she asked.

"You don't expect
me to forget,"
I answered.
"Gloom pillows."

My pillows,
like weeping willows,
had seen gallons
of tears through
the years, so I know
it sounds weird,
but I called them
gloom pillows.
They were as gray
as doom, the shades
of tombs, and some days,
soaked sopping wet.

"Maybe I'll write me a poem
or a sad, sad song
or a long sonnet
about my gloom pillows,"
I mused, pulling off
a blue pillowcase
and burying my face
in the gray.

"Hey," said Twig.
"Don't start
excavating your heart
and feeling sorry for yourself,
Laura. This is no pity

party. Sorry if I got
you started, but now stop.
This is going to be
one fun summer, and our first road
trip ever. Pick yourself up!"

Twig pounced around like a pup.

I sighed, looking at
the photo of Mom
on my closet door.
I'd gotten it blown up
as large as possible,
hoping to make
Mom life-size again.

"The Zen of death
is that she's with you,
big as ever,
every breath, every step,"
said Twig,
guessing my thoughts,
messing with the
depths of my head.

"Stop reading
my mind uninvited,"

I said.
"Quit trespassing
in my brain."

"Okay," said Twig
with a grin. There
were red cake crumbs
on her chin. "Let's write."

The silence returned,
and our muses churned.
The cool thing
about Twig and me
is that we don't need
to talk.
We can be quiet
at the same time.
No-Obligation Conversation.

I was writing poems.
Twig was writing poems.

My lava lamp rolled
slow and relaxing
like the melting wax
of an old Christmas candle
lit for the Fourth of July.

"We might be white,
but we can write
like soul sisters,
man," said Twig, doodling
and chewing on the eraser
of her pencil.

"Listen to this," she said.
"The title is 'Revolution.'"
Then she read:

You say you want a revolution,
but the Constitution
and John Lennon are dead.
Yoko Ono's alone in the bed,
shaking her head over something
John said Yesterday. What a mess today.
I Want to Hold Your Hand,
somebody or anybody's hand.
Do you have a Ticket to Ride?
I lost mine, when John Lennon died.

I applauded.
"It's just like you,"
I said. "Political
and totally cynical."

"Well, you know
I've been a Beatles
groupie since I
was a fetus," Twig
said, "thanks to
my mother playing
records to her
pregnant stomach."

Twig's parents are
eccentric. Way flaky.
Her mother does Botox
and her dad's always in detox
for one substance or another.

"I'm beside myself
for this gig," Twig said.
"Can you dig it?
Our words are big,
Sister. They stick
like burrs in the skin.
I can't wait for the
slam to begin."

Twig had this
smug mug of a
satisfied face,

and she was
wearing a chaste
pitch-black
lace dress: the best
poet's dress, I must confess.

The rest of her getup
consisted of fishnets,
a Wish Upon a Star
hat from Disneyland,
a ring on every finger
of her hands, and Twig's
favorite Chuck Taylor
sneakers: high-top
black and white.

I myself was a mess,
with a bird's nest
of bed head, elastic-
waist imitation leather
pants, a feather headband,
and a red polyester vest.

I wear lots of vests
because they are best
for hiding my breasts,
which are the size of Texas.

I was hexed and vexed
by the size of my chest,
which brought
too much negative
attention from pests.

All of a sudden,
I knew what my
first slam poem
should be about,
and I shouted
it out in the quiet
of my room:
"Gloom Pillows
and Huge Boobs!"

Twig looked at me
like I was crazy.

But baby, I knew this was it.
I'd be the hit of the gig
in Tin Can, New Jersey:
the first-prize surprise of a
big-bosomed poet chick,
quick as a whip with words.
Maybe I'd get a silver trophy
or a golden medallion

or a wad of cash or
a flashy engraved plaque
with my name on it.

But mainly,
I wanted to get revenge
on the royal pains
from my gym bench
(by being better and
more famous than them),
and also to remember
Mom and how I cried
into my gloom pillows
when she died,
and for a long time after.

Never Run from Hitting a Pig

Packing my Firebird
with all the happy crap
of two hip-hoppin',
poetic rap girls,
we hung strands
of pink pearls
from the radio knobs.
It was kind of like
a Mardi Gras bash
(except Twig and I
didn't plan to flash
anything at anybody).

"How do you like my bag?"
I asked Twig. She gave
me the thumbs-up sign.

"It's fine," she said.
"Girly pink. Sensible,
yet feminine."

My suitcase was an old
My Little Pony bag that
Mom gave me when I was eight
and taking ballet class.
My ass hadn't danced since then.

"On the road again," Twig sang
as we threw junk
into the trunk of the car.

Pops added gas cans,
jumper cables, and tools,
which I wouldn't know
how to use anyway.

"Laura," said Pops,
"maybe you should just
stay in Banesville,
where I know you're safe."

"Don't worry, Pops.
That's what cops

are for," I said,
hoping to reassure him.

"Safe is a state
of mind," added Twig.

"You don't have to go,
you know," Pops said. "Minds are
made to be changed."

"That would be wrong,"
I said. "It would be
like a song without music.
Like a gong without the boom.
It would be the ultimate of doom,
to stay here where we don't belong!"

Pops sighed.
He tried to smile.

"Pops," I said, "I'm now
an official graduate of
twelve years of torture
in Banesville High,
which was the low point
of my entire life. It's
time to come alive."

Twig slapped me five.
"Yeah," she said.
"We'll be driving
into the so-cool
School of Real Life.
The College of Reality!
The University
of Gray Road, Blue Sky,
and Yellow Lines.
A free ride."

Pops cleared his throat.
"It's not exactly free," he said.
"Don't forget who's financing
this trip. Remember the loan?"

"How could we forget my
rockin' pops with the generous
wallet?" I said. "And Twig's
gram? You're the sponsors
for Sister Slam, Twig, and the
Poetic Motormouth Road Trip.
We're going to be a big hit!"

"Please be careful," Pops said.
"You're still my little girl, you know."

"I'm bigger than you think.
Just because I carry a pink
My Little Pony bag doesn't mean
that I'm a baby," I replied. My
voice sounded like a whine, even to me.

I climbed inside the car, settling
into the driver's seat, as Twig leaped
into the passenger side.

Pops waved good-bye
and he was brave,
keeping the tears
inside of his eyes.

"Buckle your seat belts,"
he yelled as I started
the car and moved the
gearshift from park. I
raced the engine and
peeled out of the driveway.

Surprisingly, disguised
as heartburn,
I had a slight yearning
to turn around

and stay in the town
I knew by heart.

"Laura!" hollered Twig.
"Watch where you're going!"

I swerved, just missing
a kissing couple on the
side of the road.

PDAs—Public Displays
of Affection—are accepted
after graduation, I guess. I must confess
that no boy had ever kissed me in public
or in private.

"Call me Sister Slam," I said to Twig.
"I'm Sister Slam on this trip."

Twig nodded, pressing
her hand to her chest
as if I had startled
her almost to death.
She took deep breaths.

"Relax," I said. "Kick back.
You're in the good hands

of safe Sister Slam. So just chill."

I pressed the pedal to the metal
and settled deep into the seat.

A sinful wind was blowing
through my just-dyed spikes,
and the dizzy spinning
of wheels on road felt good.

The red needle
of the speedometer
was pointing higher
than I'd ever gone before.
The roar of the motor
was like a lion,
and the steering wheel
vibrated like fate
beneath my driving-
fast hands.

"Laura," said Twig.
"Slow down."

So I did. Then I said,
"Sister Slam, Twig.
"I'm Sister Slam on this trip."

"Shut up," said Twig.
"You're already making me sick.
You're getting on my nerves
way too quick.
Maybe this trip
was a big mistake.
Maybe you should take
me home, or just dump me
somewhere along the road."

That was not like Twig:
wigging over nothing.

I slammed on the brakes,
for heaven's sake,
and the car screeched to
a stop with a whopping thump.
I turned off the ignition.

Twig's skinny arms
were crossed,
and she had this saucy
look on her face,
like she was the boss of me.

"*Whatever,*" I said, and Twig
shook her head.

"So you wanna get out,
or what?" I shouted.
Then I saw that Twig
was getting half-moon circles
beneath her blue-sky eyes.
That's Twig's warning sign
that she's about to cry.
So I apologized,
even though I hadn't done anything.

"Listen," I almost whispered.
Twig's eyes glistened.

"I'm sorry," I said.
"Don't worry. Everything's cool."

Twig uncrossed her arms.
We were parked by a farm.
The odor of pig manure
was disgusting. The car motor
ticked like a clock,
and it was hot.

"That's okay," Twig said.
"I just don't want to be dead
before I get to be twenty."

Steam was hissing
from under the hood,
and I thought:
This isn't all good.
The radiator was overheating
again, and when
I started the car,
it sizzled like a hot star.

"Darn," I breathed,
and heaved
myself from the car
so that I could check
under the hood.

It was then that I saw it:
we'd hit a pig, a big fat
hog of snorting pink.

"Holy cow!" I shouted.
"Twig! We hit a pig!"

Twig leaped out
and leaned over the pig.

"Come on. Get up," she whispered.
And the pig listened!

Just like that, the chubby thing
struggled to its hooves
and waddled off,
just like this was any
ordinary carefree day.

Twig looked at me.
I looked at Twig.
We cracked up,
doubled over
with hysterical laughter.

"Hungry for pork and beans?"
said Twig.
"Ham and greens?
Maybe some bacon?"

We climbed back into
our poetmobile, and I squealed
out, leaving rubber skid marks
on the road.

If only we'd known then
what we know now:
Mister Farmer Brown
was writing down

every letter and number
of my license plate.

First rule
of the University
of Gray Road,
Blue Sky, and
Yellow Lines is this:
Never Run from
Hitting a Pig.

Lesson 4

Don't Get Cocky with Cops

The cops stopped us
somewhere southeast
of Geasterville, Pennsylvania.

In blue uniforms,
with mirror sunglasses,
and Dunkin' Donut butts,
all two members
of the police department
of Geasterville
pulled me over.

They even used sirens
and red flashing lights,
and I wouldn't be surprised
if they'd had their fingers
on the triggers.

"I'm not exactly
America's Most Wanted,
you know," I informed
Officer Cream Puff.

He just kept writing stuff,
biting his bottom lip,
probably because he had
to really think hard
to write a ticket for this.

I got a ticket—a big ticket—
for something like reckless
endangerment of swine,
and leaving the scene
of a pig that's been hit.

"Oh, shit," I said,
dropping my head
onto the steering wheel.
"Let's make a deal.
I don't hit any more pigs,
and you don't give me
this ticket."

The officer
added something
to the ticket.

Twig hissed,
"Keep your big mouth
shut, Laura. Cockiness
will get you nowhere."

But the injustice
of him busting us
for something like this
had Sister Slam pissed.

"This," I said, "was an act of God.
It was like lightning,
or a tornado,
or an earthquake.
I didn't make that pig
go on the road.
God made him waddle
out there,
right in front of me.
There was no time to stop,
Officer.
In fact, I did stop, but
the pig was already hit."

I was in deep shit.
I should have just
kept my mouth closed.
If only I'd known.

Second rule
of the University
of Gray Road, Blue Sky,
and Yellow Lines:
Never Try to Talk Your Way
Out of a Ticket When You've
Already Admitted That You Hit the Pig.

And then the cop
got his dig.
It was almost as mean
as the cool group could be,
back in the old days
at Banesville High.

"Body for Life
is a good diet.
You should try it."

That's what he said.
I wished I were dead.
Just shoot me now,

before I hit a cow.

My jaw must have dropped
because the cop
rubbed his double chin
and tried to suck up.
"I wasn't intending to insult you.
It's just that the diet has helped me,
and I want to help others."

Oh, brother.
What a loser.
Probably a boozer, too,
when he wasn't
in that uniform.

The cop patted his gut.
"Best shape I've ever been in.
I feel great.
Now be on your way.
Don't hit any pigs."

Ha, ha. Sarcasm isn't attractive
in an officer of the law.

I took off, wheels screeching,
peeling out.

With a pout,
Twig sighed.

"I could've died," she said.

"*You?* What about me?
I need a diet."

"What a riot," Twig said,
spastic and sarcastic.
"This *is* a trip."

I bit my lip.
"Twig," I said,
"do you ever
care whether
I'm fat or thin?"

Twig grinned.
"Laura . . . I mean,
Sister Slam.
I like you just
as you are. I
even like your car."
Twig's gift
is being able to lift

my spirits
when I'm sad.

"It's bangin'
to be hangin'
with you," I said.

Then we sang along
with the radio,
which was playing
a Barenaked Ladies song.
We got most of the words
wrong. Those guys are poets.

"How far to Tin Can?"
Twig yelled to a man
at a shabby gas station
we passed.

"Hey," I said.
"We're way low
on gas." It's amazing,
all the gas
you have to buy
when you're in charge
of the trip.

I did a U-turn, quick,
showing off,
burning black rubber.

"Yee-haw," Twig yelled.
Now she was getting
into the spirit of the
thing. She flapped her arms
like wings.
"Don't hit a chicken!" she squawked.

When we got out
to fill the gas tank,
this skank of a yellow-headed,
dad-aged, cabbage-shaped
dude got really rude,
saying something crude
about my boobs.

I flicked him the middle finger,
figuring that would make him
go away.

He couldn't take a hint.
"I can't believe this," I said
to Twig.
"People in the real world

are as messed up as
kids in school.
It's bull:
all that stuff they
say in school
about maturity
and real life
will be different
and all that.
It's bogus."

The obscene geek guy
opened a lemon pie
and shoved it in his venom-trap,
chewing with his mouth open
like some kind of
Conan the Barbarian
moron.

"Fat pig," he blubbered,
his flubbery gut
bouncing as he lumbered
away.

"Dork," I responded.

That's when the retard
retaliated by bombarding
my car with his smushed-up
lemon pie.

And then I
knew Rule Number Three
of the university:
People Are Rude in the Real World, Too.

Without a clue
as to what to do,
I just turned and threw
a hunk of chewed-up gum
at the dude's fat buns.

Lucky he didn't have a gun,
because I would've been one
dead poet.

But don't you know it,
when we left the station,
Mister Hideous Lemon Pie Idiot
followed right on our tail,
never failing to turn
onto every road we followed.

Lesson 5

Expect Annoying People

The Lemon Pie Guy
followed us all the way
to Tin Can,
and man, was I mad.

"Who do you think you are?"
I called to the pathetic
maggot-gagging
dweeb
crawling out of
his yellow VW.

"I know who *you* are,
missy," said
Mister Hissy Fit,
all pissy.
"You're the poet

who doesn't know it,
but you have no chance
of winning
this slam."

"Oh, boy," I shot
back, cracking up.

Twig and I,
cackling like chickens,
followed his bubble-gum butt
and flubbery gut
into the brick building.

Registration was taking place,
and most poets were patient,
waiting in line and smiling kindly,
but Lemon Pie Guy
didn't know how to smile.
He just muttered and mumbled,
grumbling, rumbling, fumbling
in his pocket
for a pencil, and then
stumbling on something
nobody else could see.

"How annoying can one person be?"
Twig commented, and a chick
in tinted-pink glasses laughed.

"I'm going to smack his
big ugly head," I said.
It wasn't what I meant,
but I said it anyway.

"That's not nice, Laura," said Twig.
"I mean, Sister Slam.
That's not nice, Sister Slam,
to tease the man."

"It's not a man," I said.
"It's a thing.
If I could sing,
I'd have a song
about how it's just wrong
to exist in this world
if you're surly
like him."

Twig grinned.
"You're the Queen of Surly,"
she said.

"I know," I agreed.
"I am edgy."

"So write a poem," said Twig.
"Forget about Gloom Pillows
and Huge Boobs.
Write about Lemon Pie Guy."

Twig is my life raft in
every hurricane,
my Tylenol for every ache
and pain.
She saves
me from going stark-raving-crazy
insane.

"Okay," I said.
"What rhymes
with Lemon Pie Guy?"

Twig shrugged.

By that time,
Lemon Pie Guy
had disappeared
into his weirdness
somewhere,

and we didn't care where,
as long as he was out
of our stare
and our air.

How to Take Lemons and Make Lemonade

Festering with indigestion
in the Sleep Best Inn
on that night in question,
I was desperate
for the white light
of revelation
that would lead
to the creation
of the best
lemon pie poem ever,
but I was suffering
from inspiration constipation.

The slam began
at 8 A.M.
the next morning,
and I was pouring

everything I had
into writing a poem.

Twig wanted to rent
videos, but I said,
"No. Poems are groovier
than movies.
Now be quiet,
so I can think."

In the pink
stink of the
cigarette-stenched
room,
Twig was digging
the sixty-six
channels on the
television screen,
and I was as green as spinach
with frenzied envy
that her poem was finished.

"This isn't a pajama party,
Miss Smarty," I said.
"I need to think!
I'm on the brink
of wearing mink

and riding in a limousine
if I win this slam.
I want to be on the
cover of *People* magazine!
I need to be the queen
of beat,
the sweetest heat
where words are concerned.
I want to burn
ears and turn
the audience to tears.
It'll be better than
a big sale at Sears.
I want the cheers!"

Twig was miffed,
and sniffled and sniffed,
and I caught a whiff
of her being pissed
at Sister Slam.

"Twig," I said,
"we're here to compete.
I don't want to be beat.
I don't even know what the prize is,
but it's got to be sweet.
Look at all the license plates

from so many states: people
coming from all over the U.S.
for this slam."

"Okay," said Twig,
and she lifted her chin.
"Write your poem.
I'll leave you alone."

She turned off the television
and made the decision
to mope. I hoped that
she'd be quiet now, but Twig sighed
and sniffed and flipped around.
The bed creaked
and Twig moaned,
sending me into
an irritation zone.

Twig huffed,
and I'd had enough.

I couldn't cope,
and my insides twisted
like old rope.

"Why," I cried,
"can't I have peace and quiet?
Let's just try it."

Twig sniffed
and hugged the pillow
to her nose,
and I wrote:

Lemon Pie Guy,
with your pee-yellow hair dye,
gut pudged as uncut pork pie:
the judges won't fudge,
so don't begrudge my win,
buzzing like a cussing
fruit fly,
Mister fly-by-night,
bow-tied, bone-dry
poet.
This is my war cry,
my psychic black eye,
indivisible, with liberty
and justice for me.
You see,
Mister Lemon Pie Guy,
my money supply
isn't high enough

to buy this contest,
so I'll win it honestly,
with supersonic
phonics, Mister Moronic.

Twig snickered.
"It sucks," she said,
and then she went
to bed.

I didn't care
what she said.
It was PMS
in the Sleep Best Inn
when Twig acted
like that.
She was a brat
about once a month.

I needed to practice,
even though Twig
was as prickly as cactus.

I also needed some Tums
to calm my stomach,
so I made up my mind
to find a vending machine

and to practice like a fiend
in the wobbly-chaired lobby
of this roach motel.

Proud as a peacock
in my old, holey-toe socks
and funky monkey nightgown,
I made my way down the
dark halls of puke-green walls.

This took balls:
walking alone
in a place
so far from home.

I'd made lemonade
from venomous lemons,
and I was the Queen of Beat,
the feminine
go-get-'em
winner of the slam
tomorrow.

Whispering my poem
as I swished along
the halls, I had a vision
of Pops

and wished
to call him.

Homesick or Pops-sick
was not an option
on the Poetic Motormouth Road Trip.
What was I:
a wimp? a gimp? Then,
limp with missing Pops,
and Mom,
and my toad-colored
bedroom at home,
I slumped on the
cracker-crumbed
floor by a snack
machine, bummed,
and way too alone.

Never Start a Slam
Without a Cup of Coffee

The sunrise
in the morning
hurt my eyes,
and I couldn't
disguise my disgust.

"Look at the dust
in this light.
And look:
these musty cheap curtains
won't even bleepin' close right!
What a bite:
eighty-nine dollars a night
just to sleep
a few hours
and take
a ten-minute shower."

"Don't complain,"
Twig moaned
and flopped over.

"We're going to need jobs,
or more money from Pops,
at this rate. I hate
how quick money runs leakin'
down the freakin' drain!"

"Don't be such a pain," Twig muttered.

I must confess
that I wasn't in the best
of moods.

"What's up with you?" Twig said.
"Better get your head
together, whether
you want to or not,
or you don't have a shot
at this contest."

I rummaged, grumbling,
through my old suitcase,
manic with panic:
a certified nut case.

"I swear,
I don't know what to wear.
I shouldn't care,
because it's not about clothes,
I know."

Twig just shook her head.

"Why do I have to be so fat?"
I asked.
"I don't want to be like that!"

"Laura," said Twig,
"you're cool,
just the way you are."

"I guess it'll be the ever-popular
polyester vest," I said,
wrestling a red vest
from a nest of messed-together threads.

"Red is your color," hollered Twig.
"Like fire. Sister Slam will lift you higher!"

"Liar," I said. "You're just saying that
to make me feel good."

"Look," said Twig,
"if you don't lose the mood,
I'm quitting this gig.
I can get a lift
and whiz
right back to Banesville."

It made me quit bitching,
to think of Twig hitching
a ride and leaving me alone.

"Let's start over," I said.
"I'm sorry. I need coffee.
I need eggs. I need ham.
Never start a slam
without grub."

We went for breakfast
in a grease-messed restaurant
next to the Sleep Best Inn.

The waitress was brooding
and rude, but at least she brought food,
and the coffee
was sweet and steamy
with sugar and cream.

"This seems
like a dream!" I said,
sipping, slurping,
burping, wishing
for the position
of Slammer
Number One
at the Tin Can
Poetry Slam.

I was ablaze
and out of my
haze, unfazed,
and crazed to
begin my win.

Lesson 8

Always Check Out the Judges Before a Slam

It was close to slam time,
and I waited in line, shiny as a dime,
ready to word-whip whiny Lemon Pie Guy
and all the other hopeful poets. Most were
younger than thirty, and some were flirty.
There were girls in low-cut shirts
and hip-hugging jeans, exhibiting cleavage
and thongs.

"That's just wrong," I whispered
to Twig. "They think they're going to win
if the judges are dirty old men."

Jumpy-grumpy
with an overdose of caffeine,
pumped with adrenaline,

I felt almost lean
and way too close to mean.

"Ssh," I said
to the socializing people
woozy and schmoozing
in a conference room
reeking of cheap perfume.
I was oozing competition:
a magician wishing
for the best rabbit trick.
I made a stage
in my mind
and practiced the lines
of my Lemon Pie Guy masterpiece.

Nervousness ceased,
and I was a beast:
the Queen of the Slam
about to begin.

Twig and I were
slam virgins, having
never been alone on stage
before. This would
be our first burst
into the world of

performance, which
was enormous.

We went into the slam room,
which was just another
gloomy conference room, with
carpet as stiff as the bristles of
a broom,
air-conditioned cool as a tomb,
with Ruffles chips crushed
into the rug.
The competitors were nervous,
and they bit their lips,
nibbled on fingernails,
and shuffled and whispered
in muffled voices.

Aluminum folding chairs
were lined in close rows, facing
one microphone standing alone
on a stage that looked like
plywood. I hoped it would
hold my weight, as I waited
for my name to be announced.
A lady wearing floral print flounced
to the stage and bounced around,
chirping, "Welcome to the

Tin Can Poetry Slam!
Poets will perform
in alphabetical order,
backward. No merciless
heckling or cursing at
competitors. The prizes
will be surprises. First
contestant: Ed Zedman."

Ed Zedman was a dead man,
pale and boring.
I was almost snoring.

Then came Sarah Yahn,
who bombed, stuttering,
fluttering the air
with words that
meant nothing.

Next was Twig,
and I was big
enough to wish
her luck.

"Break a leg, Twig,"
I whispered

as she swished in fishnets
to the front of the room.

Twig did
her "Revolution" poem,
and a heckler booed:
pollution in the room.

I clapped and cheered,
snapping my fingers
like those old Beat poets
back in the sixties.

Twig took a bow
and then sat down.
I looked around,
and the man who'd hounded
Twig was picking his nose.
"Gross," I said. "That's just
crude, dude."

Twig put her hand
over my mouth.
"Don't be so rude.
It ruins the mood."

Two hours later,
it was finally
my turn to burn, churning words
like milk into butter,
like ice cream
in the freezer.

Some geezer observer
had the nerve
to make a smart remark
about the size of my chest,
and it was a test
of my temper to ignore
the simple pimple-nosed
old fart.

I bebopped up
to the front,
and took a deep breath,
and pushed out my chest.

At the top of my lungs,
I shouted out my poem,
screaming, keeping the beat
of the sentences
with bounces of my chest
and with the rest of me.

My fat was moving, grooving,
all in one direction,
and there was no correction
because I made no
mistakes, baby.

Sweating, forgetting
my flesh, I almost
wet my pants
with the dance
of Sister Slam.

Hoarse by the time
I finished yelling,
my leg flesh turned to Jell-O,
and I noticed a flash of yellow
hair in the judges' stand.

It wasn't just any old man:
it was the obnoxious, cocky
Lemon Pie Guy. The other
judges looked just like him:
old as mold, cold-shouldered,
with hearts like boulders.

My face red
as raspberry-cherry

Kool-Aid,
I made my way
back to my seat,
where I knew
that I'd been beat.

"Geez," I hissed
to Twig,
"Sister Slam missed
this one.
I messed up big!"

"That's why," said Twig,
"you should be nice.
Take my advice
with a grain of rice,
but I think that mean words
are like head lice: they ice
the judges so much
that you'd never win
with words like that,
even if they weren't
about him."

My eyes brimmed,
and on a whim,
I hugged Twig.

"I'm sorry," I said.
"I've been a moron.
I'm going to work
harder at being smarter
before I talk
so stupid."

My voice squeaked
like chalk
on a board.

"You can't afford
to blurt out words
like puke, rebuking
everybody who rubs
you the wrong way,"
Twig said.

I nodded,
my body heavy.

"Rule Number Four
of this most-hip road trip,"
whispered Twig.
"Always check out the judges
before a slam."

Always Check the Gas Tank Before Leaving

We checked out
of the Sleep Best Inn
and headed
for the rotten-egg-scented
parking lot.

"Laura, your car!"
shouted Twig.

Somebody had written
witless shit, scribbled
in dribbled soap on the doors:
FATTY'S ROAD TOURS, it said.

I just shook my head.
Some people needed
to get a life.

I noticed that a bunch of
hunched-over pre-teenyboppers
were cracking up,
cackling hysterically
until they practically rolled
on the ground.

"Yo," I yelled.
"Sticks and stones
can break my bones,
but words will never
hurt me."

I was lying.

I pried
my eyes wide,
trying to look
cruel, but it was bull,
because I knew
I looked like a fool.

Twig played it cool.
She waved like a
beauty queen,
like Miss Teen America—
a barracuda of coolness—

like she was riding in a
lime-green limousine,
or inside a fine convertible.

"Let's make an excellent exit;
don't hex it,"
she whispered,
and we drifted sexily
in the direction
of my 1969 Firebird,
ignoring the door words.

We threw our suitcases
into the backseat,
gleaming, beaming
screamingly fake smiles.

I stared straight ahead,
at the steeple of a Jersey church,
and pretended that God
was throwing rocks
at the jerks, giving them
what they deserved.
The nerve of some people
who call themselves human.

I was fuming
and started the car
by racing the accelerator.
We left
the Sleep Best Inn
of Tin Can
with a squeal of wheels,
leaving rubber
skid marks
in the parking lot.

I laughed fearlessly
at the sight of the weirdos
in my rearview mirror.

"Good-bye and good riddance!"
I said. "Hope we never meet again."

Then Twig said,
"Where to next?"

"I don't know.
Let's just blow
this clown town
and hit the road."

"Laura," said Twig,
"I mean, Sister.
We can't afford to
waste gas.
You know, we're low
on cash."

"Nah," I said.
"Don't fret."

But just then,
with a sputter
and a mutter
and a flutter
of a cough,
the gas tank
of my poor old car
went empty,
which was exactly
the most embarrassing
exit we ever
could have made,
one-eighth
of a mile
from the Sleep Best Inn.

"But we just got gas yesterday," Twig
complained.

"Only eight," I said. "I put only eight
dollars in."

"Oh, that'll get us way far," Twig said.

So Twig and I set our sights
on the Exxon station,
making a vacation
of walking a mile
down the highway,
gas cans in our hands,
leaving the laughing people behind.

Never Let Your Best Friend Attack Your Sanity and Your Vanity

By the time
we came back,
Twig had gas
on her hands
and a bug
up her butt.
She wouldn't speak
to me.

"This is ridiculous, Twig,"
I said,
and she put her hands
over her ears.

"Now your ears
just smell

like gasoline,
too, Miss Poo-Poo Mood,"
I said.

Twig started to hum.
It's so dumb
when she does that.
She was humming
the "Star-Spangled Banner,"
mangling, strangling
the notes.

"I think it's sacrilegious
to our country to hum
our national anthem
when you're
Miss Temper Tantrum,"
I said to Twig.

She ignored me,
pouring the gas from
her can
into the tank
of the car.

"Ooo-kay, have it your way,"
I said.

Cars were honking
as they passed by,
but nobody even tried
to find out if we needed help
or anything like that.

There we were,
one fat, one skinny:
two chicks
with an out-of-gas
Firebird plopped
along the side
of the road
in Jersey.

Twig finished with the gas
and threw her can
into the trunk.
Then the punk
flopped into the
backseat,
propped up her feet,
and crossed her arms,
the Queen of Charms.

Not frazzled,
just slightly hassled,

I nozzled gas
into the tank, thankful
that I wasn't
as cranky as Miss Skanky.

Then she went psycho,
and for some crazy reason
kicked the back of
my car seat.

"Get over it," I hissed.
Now I was pissed.
Twig just missed
being hit by the gas can
when I tossed it
onto the back floor.

I started the car
and took off with a roar:
the chauffeur of a backseat loafer
with a bad attitude.

"It's really rude
to sit in the back,
like I'm some kind
of taxicab hack.
You crack

me up, Twig.
Well, actually,
I'm not laughing.
I'm mad. This is bad.
Way sad. My best friend
on the planet
acts manic-depressive
on me, which isn't
impressive to me.
What are you,
bipolar or something?
You're acting
like your mom,
going through menopause."

Twig snapped.
"Don't talk about my mom!
At least *she*
doesn't hit pigs
or get tickets
or throw bubble gum
at the butts
of lemon pie guys
who turn out
to be judges
who hold grudges.
She doesn't do stuff

like get all huffy
just because
she needs a cup of coffee,
or needs to write some mean-
spirited poem about
the judge of the contest
she wants to win.
My mom doesn't spin
her tires leaving parking lots,
like that's going to get her
attention or a mention
in the newspaper or something.
My *mom* doesn't run
out of gas like some dumbass.
She's not a crazy lunatic
in a polyester vest,
thinking she's the best
at everything she attempts."

That did it.
Twig's words
were the straws
that broke
the Sister's back:
a personal attack
on my sanity
and my vanity

and my driving
and the jiving
of my words.
I was burning,
turning hotter
under the collar
as my heart
pounded harder
and harder.

I tried to
make my mind reason
with my temper, but it
didn't work.

I slammed, rammed
on the brakes,
making the car
scream to a
way-too-sudden
neck-wrenching stop.

I hoped
there was
no cop.

I took a fast breath,
filling my chest
with the air
of regret
that you get
when your very best friend
rips your skin
with sentences
that'll never mend anything.

I twisted
the friendship ring
off my finger,
remembering
how Twig had given
it to me
for Christmas
the year we met.
I still wet my bed,
when we met.
I was nine,
and Mom had
just died.
Twig was my favorite savior
that year.
Ever after,
we were glued at the hips:

two chicks indivisible.
Inseparable,
until now.

"Get out," I said.
"If you don't like
me, just get out of the car.
Walk. Hitchhike.
Buy a bike.
Go home to your mom,
who's more perfect
than me, thanks to
the wonders of Botox
and cosmetic surgery."

I held my breath,
hoping that she wouldn't go.

But she did. Twig
flipped her hair
like she didn't care
about anything but herself,
as if she had her own club
of people who
worshipped her,
and then she leaped

out of her seat
and through the door.

"Good-bye," she said.
"Have a nice life."

Then Twig reached in
and lifted her suitcase,
sifting her face
into a blank slate,
the colorless
shade of
squid-squishy
fish bait.

I almost hated her then:
my ex–best friend.

"Been nice knowing you," she said.
"Most of the time."

And then Twig climbed
up a little thicket on a hill
by the side of the road,
sticking her thumb
in the hick-thick air
and not looking back.

Tears streaming
down my cheeks,
I put the car in drive,
feeling less alive
than ever before in my life,
leaving my friend behind.

Lesson 11

Expect That Some Things Will Be Crappy

Five miles later,
I no longer hated her,
so I turned around
and found
Twig, still hitching,
her dumb thumb
in the air.

Weak with relief,
and frantic,
I screamed.

"Don't you care
that you could get
yourself killed?
Get in the car,
you retard,

before some creepy
brainless maniac
keeps you forever
shivering, starving
in the batty attic
of some old house
in Jersey."

Twig tried not to smile.
She bit her lip.
She threw out her hip,
and her fishnets were ripped.
She turned down her mouth.
She scowled,
but it didn't wow me.

I knew
that she'd been crying.
Twig is no good at lying
to me,
even if she doesn't say
a word.

"You're a spaz," she said.
"I can't believe
that you'd leave
me by the side of a road

somewhere in Jersey.
What a jerk
you can be."

Twig ran fast
and opened the door.

"But I like you anyway.
I'm really sorry for the
stuff I said. Still friends?"
Twig said.

I thought for a second,
just messing
with her head.
"I guess," I relented
with a grin.

Twig got in.
"I'll just forget
that this incident
happened. It was a bunch
of crap. It wasn't my bad;
it wasn't your bad.
Too much togetherness,
I guess."

"Two poets on the road," I said,
"can't always be happy.
Sometimes things will be crappy.
But don't get all sappy.
Let's rap, and slap the map
northward. Let's move forward.
The bad stuff is done.
Let's move on:
Sister Slam, Twig,
and the Poetic
Motormouth Road Trip!
Let's rip!"

"Where to next?" Twig asked.

We were two crazy
ladies like in that movie
Thelma and Louise.
We could go anywhere,
without a care, on a dare,
baring our souls to the world.
Do anything!
We could just fling
our arms
and embrace
the universe,
filling our purses

by writing verses
that would win
every slam in America.

"So, where do we go?"
I said.
"Let's go where
all good poets go! SoHo!"

"SoHo?" Twig said.
"Like in New York City?"

"Yep!" I said,
nodding my head.
"SoHo, where all poets go,
in the city that never sleeps.
The bustling Big Apple,
where we'll cripple-crapple
all poet opponents!
We'll be boho in SoHo.
Ho-ho-ho and a bottle of rum.
You'll wear a neon-pink wig,
but still be Twig.
This'll be big, Twig!
What a gig.
We'll take a voyage
through the Village,

and pillage trash cans
of the best restaurants,
getting good eats for free.
It'll be easy, you'll see."

"Whoopee," said Twig,
but she didn't sound
convinced, since her voice
sounded more like a
whoopee cushion than a cheer.

"Have no fear," I said.
"We'll be like
those old Beat poets.
You know:
the finger-snapping,
happenin' dudes,
except we're chicks,
from the sticks
of Banesville, Pennsylvania.
We'll be famous.
We'll have our pictures
on the front page
of the *New York Times*:
The Queens of Rhymes!"

"Give me time," said Twig,
"to think about this.
How will we exist
without money?"

"Honey," I replied,
my eyes on the highway,
"you just leave it to me."

"You know," said Twig,
"the living is big
in New York.
A pork sandwich or a Manwich
costs six bucks or so."

"Don't lecture," I said.
"Don't worry your furry head.
Just enjoy the trip."

Snippy as a whip,
Twig snapped open a map.

"You're full of crap," she said.
"But let's go. SoHo, here we come."

And then, she started to hum.

Lesson 12

Don't Look at Your Hair While Driving

Confused in Newark,
New Jersey,
blurry-eyed and tired,
I drove
over and over
in a cloverleaf
of jerky circles:
around and around
the airport area.

"We're bound
to get out
of this eternal circle
sometime," I said.

I sneaked a peek
at my hair
in the rearview mirror.

It was wrong, way wrong,
not to pay attention.

That's when it happened:
my bumper was just
tapping the fender
ahead of mine.
It wasn't a crime,
just a little fender bender,
not the end of the universe,
but of course, Twig was
a nervous wreck.

Heck, it was nothing
to be frothing or
shouting about.
Fender benders are
common denominators
in Newark, New Jersey,
where people drive crazy.

We pulled over
to the side of the road—

where loads
of traveler's trash
was dumped,
and so was the old
hunk of junk
that I'd bumped. Actually,
just *tapped*.

I almost crapped
when this not-quite-male,
not-quite-female bailed
out of the car I'd nailed.

He/she was decked out
in a glitzy ditzy itsy-bitsy
prissy pink dress
with pearls. Swirls
of curly furled hair
showed through the nude
pantyhose on his toes
and legs. He was wearing,
I swear, a Rapunzel wig
from the Disney Store,
or somewhere.

If he'd had a sparkly wand,
he could have been

a twin of the tooth fairy,
hairy legs and all.

"Leave it to you," hissed Twig.
"Your fender bender
had to be with a gender bender."

"Ssh," I said.

The Newark Tooth Fairy
teetered and tottered
in too-high spiked heels,
and leaned down in his nifty little
glittery gown with not a hint
of a frown.

"It's only a homely
old Pinto," he said,
waving his hand.
"A rusty fusty
old bucket of bolts.
No damage.
Don't worry about it,
girlfriend. It's not worth
the expense of an
insurance increase."

"Geez," I wheezed.
My knees were knocking,
rocking with
choked-back hysteria.

I blushed, or flushed,
got goose bumps,
and then gushed
with so much
appreciation.
It was my initiation
into the world of weird.

"We are way far
from home,"
I pronounced
as Mister Pink Dress
flounced away,
swaying, sashaying.

"Yeah," said Twig.
"We're not in Kansas
anymore, Toto.
We're not even
in SoHo."

"It went without a hitch," I said.
"Just a glitch, a tiny stitch
on the fabric map of where
we're going."

"Speaking of maps,"
Twig said, "are you lost?"

"I'm the boss," I said.
"Hold onto the hoss, cowgirl,
because we're almost
in New York."

With those words,
I made some tight right
turns as a fly-by bird
splattered a
shattered souvenir
of Newark smack-dab
in the middle
of the windshield.

Maybe that's why
I missed the YIELD
sign.
Or maybe it was
the sun

in my eyes.
Or the fact
that I couldn't stop
cackling about
the pink-dress
guy.

I don't know why,
but in the blink
of a winking
eye,
my Firebird
was smashed,
crashed,
bashed
on the driver's side
full force
by a Mustang
that was no dang horse.

When the universe
stopped spinning,
I thought maybe
I was dead
and in heaven.
But then again,
my wrecked head

was dizzy
and fizzy from
the crash.

Twig groaned,
and I heard the
ding-a-ling ring
of a cell phone.

"I guess this isn't heaven," I said.
"You don't need
to call people
when you're dead."

Twig and I kicked
wickedly
with our Doc Marten
boots,
pushing
our way
through
the ruckus-buckled
doors,
and the roars
of traffic
whooshing,
rushing,

whizzing past,
hissing,
blasted fast
into my head.

"What the heck
is up with all
these accidents?"
Twig asked,
and I shrugged.

"Beats me," I said.

"Are you sure
we're not dead?"
Twig asked.
"All I saw was blue,
coming at you. Whew!"

Twig's knee was bleeding,
tiny droplets of blood leaking
through her skin.
I didn't know where to begin
figuring out how the crash happened.

"What the hell?"
somebody yelled.
"Everybody all right?"

I saw the white light
of fight, and was in
the mood for super-bad attitude.

"How rude!" I shouted,
but then doubted
my sanity and bit
my lip when I
caught a glimpse
of the cute dude
in the blue Mustang.
Dang, he was hot.
A lot. We don't
often see good-looking
guys in the boondocks
of Banesville.

I stuttered,
words spreading like butter,
heart fluttering,
muttering something
about how manically
sorry I was

to have blurted
impulsive stuff
to such a hunk.

I was such a punk.

The guy's eyes
were kind of like
green lime, except sweet.
Avocado-hotto green,
the shade of Kool-Aid
with sugar.

I'm a sucker
for hunky guys
with green eyes,
and was suddenly
struck shy.

"Hi . . . wh . . .what's
your name?"

I was so lame.
My claim to fame
isn't playing the game
of flirtation.
The sensation

of numbness
and dumbness
made my brain
fall asleep.
I was a geek.
I was weak
in the speaking
department.

"My . . . my
name is
Laura,"
I mumbled,
stumbling, fumbling
for something
not bumbling.

"Sister Slam
on this trip,"
said Twig,
and I jabbed
her with
my elbow.

"Oww!" howled Twig.

The guy smiled,
and his teeth
were like a
tooth whitener
commercial,
or an ad in a magazine.

I was smitten, bitten
by a love bug
or something.
I didn't
even care
that I'd
just been hit.

I was in deep smit.

Lesson 13

Always Be Ready to Be Struck by the Love Bug

My car (it had been Mom's car, too,
which made me kind of blue)
was totaled, and a passing tow truck
stopped to hook it up.
Soon, they'd be taking my Firebird
away to the Graveyard
of Crashed Cars.

I had a vision that my car
would rest in peace,
and that at least
I would get
a big insurance settlement
from the wreck.

"How are you
getting home?"

asked the guy
of the sweet green eyes,
and I shrugged.

The love bug
affected my tongue,
and I clung to Twig's arm.
I was charmed,
struck speechless.

"We're going
to the city," said Twig.

"Me, too," the guy said.
"I live near here,
but I'm meeting my parents
for a week of vacation."

I still couldn't speak.

"You're, like, eighteen," Twig said,
"and you still go on trips
with your parents?"

The guy shrugged.
I could have hugged
him; that's how cute the dude was,

with duck fuzz on his chin
where a goatee should have been.

"Hey," he said,
"we stay at the Waldorf,
okay? It's cool.
I'd be a fool
to turn down a free week
at the Waldorf-Astoria."

I was filled
with euphoria.
This was phantasmagoria:
a dream come true.

Not only was he
cute, but the dude
had bucks. It sucks
not to have bucks.

"What luck!" I said.
"It's a coincidence!
That's kind of like
where we're going, too!"

"Laura," said Twig.
"What about SoHo?"

"Oh, no. No SoHo.
Waldorf all the way. Hey!
Do you have room for two more?
We'll sleep on the floor."

"Sure," said the guy.
"My parents won't mind."

I started to climb
into his car.

"Laura!" said Twig.
"We need to wait
for the police.
And at least
you should know his name,
for heaven's sake!"

"Jake," he said.

I liked the shape
of Jake's head:
big enough to hold
a good brain.

"It's great;
it totally rates

to make your acquaintance,
Jake," I said.

Manners are a banner
advertising a good upbringing,
so I shook his hand.
Man, it was electric,
metric-system mathematics
full of static shocks
when our eyes locked.
One plus one equals two
out-of-the-blue
in love, or lust, busted.

Twig was disgusted.
She sighed
and rolled her eyes.

Jake had two
ear hoops
and a fine tattoo
of a Chinese
squiggle-symbol
on his arm.

"You look like
a poet, don't
you know it?" I said.

Jake smiled,
and I went wild inside.

"A musician," he said.
"Guitar strummer, drummer,
writer of songs."

"You can't go wrong," I said.

Twig just shook her head.

"A drummer," she said.
"What a bummer.
Remember the Mummers
in the Philadelphia parade?
I would've paid
those drummers to shut up."

I was mortified,
embarrassment fortified
by Twig's wacked
lack of respect for Jake.

Sirens shrilled,
and I could have killed
Twig. I willed
myself filled
with a balm of calm.

"Here come the cops,"
said Twig. "Hey, maybe
they'll throw us in jail.
It never fails,
in the movies,
that the groovy
people end up
in jail, no bail."

"We're not going
to prison," I said.

The officer wore dark shades,
and he asked our names,
butt-strutted around to
look at our plates,
then got on his radio
walkie-talkie thing
to call in to somebody
who cared about stuff
like this.

Static crackling,
the officer started cackling
when he heard
that I got a ticket
for hitting a pig.

I don't know how
you get a gig
where you can make a big
deal out of stuff like this.

But he did.

"Kid," said the cop,
"you have too many
Pennsylvania points
on your license. By
the way, I need to see
your license."

"It's in the glove compartment
of that crushed car over there,"
I said, and the officer shook his head.

"Is she going to prison?"
Twig asked.

The officer shook his head.

"You should've just stayed in bed
this morning,
because you've crashed and bashed
your way
into losing
your driver's license, young lady.
It'll be revoked."

Holy smokes. I was *so* not stoked.

But then I remembered:
I didn't have wheels anymore anyway.

It was my big day.
I'd have to just ride away
into the blazing sunset with Jake.

This was no mistake.
This was fate.
My first date,
and I couldn't wait
one minute more.

Lesson 14

Always Look Your Best Because You Never Know Who You're Going to Wreck Into

Jake's car was
dented but driveable,
and I'd never
felt more alive
in my life.
I felt like fluff,
a bubble,
floating, buzzing,
no more trouble.
My senses were on
high alert, and even
though my head
and neck hurt,
I fretted about my
breath and kept

getting mint Certs
from Twig.

"Stop bumming,"
said Twig,
who was humming
the Beatles song
"Let It Be."

(I beat
her to the car,
so my seat was up
front, with Jake.)

A bundle of stress,
I sweated and fidgeted:
a midget in the
presence of greatness
with Jake-ness.

Jake had six
bags of candy
in the backseat,
and he reached
back and fished
out a bag for me:
spicy red cinnamon hearts.

"You're so nice.
I love spicy
candy," I gushed.

I wished I'd worn
some glamorous
purple eye shadow
and mascara,
so I could bat
my lashes
in a passion
of flirtation,
but I'd been too lazy
for makeup.

That proves
that it grooves
to always look
your best,
because you
just never know
who you're going
to wreck into.

I hoped that Jake
wouldn't notice
my lack of cosmetics,

and that he'd get
romantic about my
intellect instead.

I dumped a handful
of candy
into my mouth,
then shoved the bag
in the pocket
of my vest.
It was best
if I didn't invest
much attention
in sweets.
("Hi. My name
is Laura
and I'm a sugar-holic.")

The skyline of the city
shimmered, glimmered,
mysterious in the distance,
and I started to sing
that goofy old tune
"I Love New York."

Jake drove like an expert,
never once swerving.

I funneled
my emotions,
pouring out boring
words, rambling
on and on.
"So I was born
in Banesville,"
and stuff like that.
The motion of the Mustang
was a potion of relaxation,
and the sensation of floating
took over.

In the dimness
of the Lincoln Tunnel
of love, snug as
a thumb in a glove,
I hovered over
the shifter and whispered,
"You are so totally cute."

"How rude!" Twig fussed.
"That's lewd, just crude, to
swoon all moon-faced
with Jake, who you just met,
like, sixty minutes ago."

I looked at the clock.
"Eighty minutes,"
I said. "And ten seconds."

"I'm guessing that you must
be in shock," Twig said.
"Maybe we should stop
at a hospital.
A *mental* hospital."

"I might be in shock," I said,
"but Jake rocks."

"Ignore her," said Twig.
"She's not usually like this.
She's never
even kissed a guy
in her entire life."

"No way," said Jake.

"Yes way," said Twig.

"You're full of shit," said Jake.

"No way," said Twig.

"Wait a minute!" I said.
"What is this?
The *Jerry Springer* show?
My first kiss, you know,
is my business!
It'll be kismet, destiny,
what-will-be-will-be,
the best freaking ever
for me, happening
when it's meant to be."

"Maybe when
she's eighty,"
said Twig.

We shot
from the tunnel
and into the city,
and I was feeling ditzy.

"What's up,
Big Apple?
What's happenin'?"
I shouted at people
on sidewalks and streets.

It was a smorgasbord
of humanity,
and profanity
slipped from my lips.

"Holy shit!
I never saw so
many different
races in the
same place!"

It was a
rat race, a
street pace
of faces
from light
to dark
and in between:
more skin
colors
than exist
in the
white-bread world
of Banesville.

"If we look
real close,

we might
see the host
of a game show,
or a sports hero,
or a size-zero
supermodel,"
Twig said.
"We might
see the
grooviest movie
stars,
or TV stars,
or famous players
of guitars!
Who knows
who goes
in all the limos?"

Horns blared,
and nobody cared
or stared
or dared to bare
their teeth
in the hint of
a grin.

I didn't know
where to begin
to look.
"I could
write a book
of poems
about this city,"
I said.

I felt New York
in my bones
and in my flesh:
a mishmash mesh
of a place
that starts
the race
for the rest
of America.

"This is just
like you see on TV!"
I said. Jake just
smiled and shook his head.

I was in a state
of hysteria, laughing and staring,
not even caring

what Jake thought,
or thinking that I ought
to be cool.

Jake played
tour guide, driving
fearlessly in bumper-to-
bumper craziness, unfazed.

"Here we are!"
Jake announced,
proud. "The Waldorf-
Astoria, to your left."
Jake coasted
to the sidewalk.

"Is this where you park?"
I asked, in the dark
about how a car gets
parked in a place like this.

Jake shook his head.
"Parking garage," he said.

It was like a ballet:
a valet and a mellow
yellow-tasseled bellboy

and a top-hatted, tailcoated
doorman, all in a dance
of service just for us.

They made such a fuss,
tipping their caps
and zapping us with happy
smiles and all that.

I felt so fat,
and not quite
dressed right,
and tried
with all my might
to be polite.

Jake knew
just how to act,
not lacking in manners
or cosmopolitan coolness.

He opened
the trunk, looking like
such a hunk, and lifted
a guitar case from inside,
along with a cool blue suitcase.

"I'll get your bags,
miss," said the
whistling bell guy,
and it was then
that I realized
that . . . *Duh!*
Twig and I
were so totally dumb,
and our suitcases
(and wallets)
were on their way
to the place
where wrecked cars go.

Never Wash Your Face in the Bidet

"You can borrow my clothes,"
said Jake as we waited
for the elevator.

"Thanks, but what size?
Don't lie. Your pants
don't have a chance
of fitting my ass," I said.
"And Twig's too skinny."

"My mom's a stick," Jake said.
"Her stuff will fit Twig.
And my dad's big.
I mean, slightly large.
Or you could just
charge your credit card
and buy a whole bunch

of new clothes,
like at Saks or Macy's
or somewhere."

I sighed. I could
have died. My wide
load was so fat
that it'd compare
to someone's *dad*.
This was bad. Way sad.
So I just tried to laugh.

"Can you believe
how brainless
we were, to leave our
bags in the car!"

I didn't want
to confess that I didn't possess
a MasterCard or Visa
or any other plastic money.
Pops was funny about stuff
like that, and never allowed
me to apply for credit cards.
"The interest will get the best
of you," he always said.

But now my head was exploding.
I had no clothes to wear.
I'd have to be a nudist
in New York.
What a doofus of a dork.

The Waldorf was the fanciest
hotel I'd ever been in.
I couldn't believe
we were going to sleep here.
The lobby alone put my home
to shame. I felt lame,
such a mess in my polyester vest
over a 1970s dress, bopping across
the lobby in scuffed-up
combat boots. Everybody else
was cute or rich: bitchy rich.
A lady in the lobby,
wearing a mink,
with a pink hat,
wouldn't even bat
her snobby eyes at us.

"What's up with *that?*
A mink coat
in the month
of June?"

Twig said
way too loud.

We didn't
know how to act
in a place like this.

I was pissed
that I hadn't dressed up
in something nice,
since I'd have to wear
it for the rest of my life.

The elevator came,
and I was so lame,
I just let Jake
push the button
for Forty-Four
and then sank to
the floor as we soared
to the sky.

"Are you
all right?"
asked Jake.

"Stomachache.
I'm afraid
of heights."

"What a
bite," Jake said.
"Wait until
you see the view
from our room."

Impending doom
in my womb,
I just clutched
my stomach
and moaned.

"Laura," said Twig,
"get a grip."

When the elevator
finally came
to a stop,
I mopped
the sweat from my head
and caught
a glimpse
of myself

in the
golden mirror.
I was
a freaking mess.
I hated
this outdated dress,
and the vest
didn't do much
to hide my breasts.

"To the left,"
Jake said. He led
us down the hall.
The walls were so
elegant. I was
an elephant. Even the
paintings were shaking
from my steps.

Jake kept walking
and walking,
and the hall felt like
forever, and Twig's
step was light
as a feather,
and I thought

we'd never
get there.

I needed Nair
for my hairy
legs. The stubble
rubbed together
when I walked.
This made me sulk,
and I didn't talk much.

I was such
a grump, a lump
of rump and legs
and breasts.
The underarms
of my dress
were wet
with sweat.

Jake came
to a stop by door
Four-Hundred
Forty-Four.

Jake opened
the door

with a plastic
key card,
and I caught
my breath.

The room wasn't just
a room. It was
a freaking suite.
We were
in the towers, and
there were flowers
and furniture everywhere.

A lady with shiny
Barbie-blonde
hair was there,
and a man
with a tropical tan.

"These are
the 'rents," Jake said.
"Vince and Misty . . .
Twig and Sister Slam."

I stuck out my hand.

"Sir and ma'am,
pleased to meet you."

Jake looked impressed.
I was on my best
behavior, because
Jake was our savior.

"Mom and Dad," he said,
"you won't believe this.
I just missed being killed
in an accident
because I wasn't
paying attention. Anyway,
the Mustang is okay,
just a few dents and
dings. The cops came,
and they took away
Twig and Sister's car,
and they're far from home
without any money
or clothes. They're poets.
So, anyway, could they
stay? Like,
on the floor?
They sure do need
a place to stay."

"Well . . . okay," said
Jake's mom.
She was the bomb.

"Have you
called your
parents?" asked
Jake's dad.

"We don't
have cell phones,"
Twig said.
"And anyway,
Laura's mother
is dead."

Twig was hit
by what she'd said.
She turned red
and put her hands on
her head.

"That didn't
come out right,"
she said.
"I mean,
she passed away,

so Laura only
has a father.
And I don't
bother much
with my parents,
because they're,
like, way into
themselves."

Misty raised
her perfectly
tweezed eyebrows,
and Vince frowned,
crinkling his brown skin.

Twig couldn't win.
Everything she said
came out wrong.

"If you call
your parents,"
Vince said,
"I'll speak
to them."

I dreaded
letting Pops know

about the wreck,
but what
the heck . . .
he had to find out
sooner or later.

A waiter-dude came
into the room,
wearing a bow tie
and holding
a silver tray
full of food.

I felt rude,
eating their food,
but Misty insisted.

"Bon appetit," she said.
"Have some
hors d'oeuvres."

The nerve
of Twig:
she just
dove right in,
helping herself

to a wealth of grub
that cost big bucks.

I was reluctant
and said, No,
thank you
very much,
that I'd already
had lunch,
but Misty made such
a big deal
out of needing
to eat
a mini-meal
in between
each big
meal that
I finally
gave in.

"It's a sin
to waste," Misty said.

I tasted
a paste
of something
expensive

spread on a
Ritz cracker,
and felt like such
a slacker,
not offering
to pay.

"So, can
they stay?"
Jake asked.

I couldn't believe
my ears,
but he really seemed
to be into Twig and me
sleeping here.

I wasn't clear as to why,
but the guy had made
up his mind to be
way kind to Twig and me.

"They may stay,"
said Vince, "if their parents
give permission.
It's their parents' decision."

"But they're eighteen,"
Jake said,
and his green
eyes gleamed.
"I have an idea.
They'll write
poems about you.
They're poets,
you know.
They'll make
you famous,
saying your
names at poetry
slams all over
this city."

"Don't be silly,"
said Misty as she
wiped her lips
on a linen napkin.
"All we ask
is their
parents' permission."

As I wished to
sink deep into a hole
in the floor, Twig heaped

more hors d'oeuvres
onto a plate, and I began
to hate her once more.
"Twig! Don't be
such a pig!"
I hissed.

"I'm starving
to death,"
Twig mumbled,
her mouth
stuffed full
of crumbled cracker.

"Look," said Jake.
"They're hungry.
They're alone
in a strange
city, with no clothes
to wear.
They don't even
have clean underwear!
Don't you care?"

"Dude," said Twig,
"you rock."

A clock
chimed five times.

"That reminds me!"
said Misty.
"Tavern on the Green!
We have reservations
for six o'clock dinner!"

"Please join us,"
said Vince. "Our treat."

I stammered,
then blabbered
and jibber-jabbered
something lame
about wishing
we could pay.

"No problem," said Vince.
"If you'd like to freshen up,
there's an extra
restroom in the next
room, through that door."

Twig finished her
pig-out feast,

and I was glad
that at least
she'd stopped eating.

We clomped
into the next
room, which
was spooky,
dark as a
tomb, with
the drapes drawn.

I yawned.
It had been
a long day.

"Hey!" said Twig.
"I bet that this
is Jake's bed."

I turned red.

Twig jumped up,
her boots on the covers.
I shuddered.

"You need
better manners," I said.

Twig jumped
up and down,
and I found
the light switch
to a rich-people
bathroom.

"Cool!" said Twig,
running in. "Look at this:
they have a little
pink sink,
to wash your face,
I think."

"Twig," I said.
"That's not a sink,
and it's not to wash
your face.
It's a bidet."

"What the hey
is a bidet?"
asked Twig.

"It's to wash places,
not faces, that are,
you know . . . *down below.*"

Twig groaned.
"Gross," she said.
"You mean like butts
and stuff?"

"Yeah," I said.
"I saw one on TV."

I could have died,
because Twig tried it
that minute.

"This is way strange,"
she said. "Rich people
have some weird
ways: *bidets* and *bon appetits*
and *hors d'oeuvres* and *caviar.*
What's up with all the
French stuff?"

The bathroom door
wasn't closed,
and all of a sudden

Jake poked his nose
into the room.
"Whoa!" he said.

"You're supposed to knock,"
Twig said, pulling up her stockings.

Jake did a dance of embarrassment,
the harassment from Twig
not helping matters.

"I'm really sorry,"
he said, blushing
as the bidet went on flushing.
"It's just that we're
rushing to get to
dinner on time."

We hadn't realized how many
minutes had raced by.

I could have died
a million times
of mortification.

I shoved a handful
of candy hearts
into my mouth.

Twig had been
so totally uncouth.

And it was then
that I lost a tooth.

Lesson 16

Be Very Careful When Chewing Hard Cinnamon Hearts

Looking at the spit-out
red blitz of cinnamon heart
bits that I spouted
into my hand,
I was having fits.
This was the pits.

The gap in my yap
zapped me into
a state of shock,
and I grabbed
a plastic shower cap,
hiding my trap,
so that the empty
eyetooth space
wasn't in full
reddish-blue

view of anybody
who looked at me.

"Let's go!" called Vince.

I winced.
I needed
assistance,
an emergency
dentist, but I had
no insurance.

"Come on,
Miss Toothless,"
teased Twig.
She could be
way crude,
too rude,
for the sake
of a laugh
from a dude.

But Jake didn't
even crack a smile.

He bent down
and gently

pulled back
the plastic shower
cap, peering
at my mouth.

"Bummer," he said.

I was on the
verge of blubber.

I flicked
the goop,
including my tooth,
into the
toilet bowl, playing
the role of Okay-ness.

"No way in this universe
can I stay
this way," I said.
"I can't go out to dinner
like this."

"Get a grip," said Twig.
"We can't miss
a meal like this.
I mean,

Tavern on the Green!
That's a
famous, groovy
movie-star place!
It'd be a disgrace
to blow off
a fancy chance
like this."

I was pissed.
Twig couldn't have
cared less
about how
embarrassed
I felt.

"Actually,"
said Jake,
tilting his head,
"you look kind
of quirky-perky
cute like that.
There are
high-throttle models
with gaps
in their teeth,
you know. I'd just

let it go. The essence
of Sister Slam
is eccentricity.
That's why I like you:
you're unique."

"You mean, like,
a geek?" I asked,
and Jake laughed.

"No way!" he said.
"You're smart and
artistic. You're no
bimbo chick, flouncing
around primping and simpering.
You're interesting."

"Me?" I asked.
"*Interesting*?"

"Yeah," Jake said.
"Different. A mix
of bizarre and
beautiful in
a psychedelic
fairy-tale-
mermaid kind

of way. Like
you're not meant
to stay
on the dirt
of Earth.
Like you
belong in
blue air, or
the water."

"Like Flubber?" I asked.

"No," he said.
"I never meant
that. Don't
you know
how to take
a compliment?"

Jake's face
was sincere,
clear as a star,
and I gasped,
falling hard and
fast, stumbling into
something like
a crush, gushing love
for Jake.

Part of me
couldn't believe
this stroke
of pixie-dust luck,
and I felt as if
I'd been
struck by a
Pizza Hut
delivery truck
or a hockey puck.
I was a sitting duck.

Without thinking, I said,
"You're the nicest guy
I've ever met
in my entire life."

Jake grinned,
and dimples
creased his cheeks.

I made up my mind
that I'd try to become
the person Jake saw.

"Let's go," I said.

When we stepped
out of the hotel,
someone had cast
a magic spell,
and I let out a yell,
because there was a limousine
with a driver
named Miguel.
I felt like a
southern belle,
or a pearl
pried from
an oyster shell.
I felt like
the Queen
of Caffeine
or the Cocoa
Bean, like I owned
an automatic
teller machine.
Dressed in
my Halloween-tangerine
1970s dress, this
felt like a dream.
I was not serene:
I was a Mexican
jumping bean.

"Yippee!" I shrieked.

The limousine
was a sleek bright white,
and it stretched elegantly,
luxuriously long.

Nothing more could go wrong.

I climbed into
the limousine,
and it was the
coolest car I've
ever seen:
tinted windows,
shimmery bottles
of expensive wines
for the kinds
of people who dress
fine, and champagne.
It was raining,
but we were
in a moon-white cocoon
of luxury.

"Wish I had
the bucks

for wheels
like this,"
I whispered
to Jake.

He smiled, and his eyes
were like Easter-lily vines:
aquamarine seas just for me
to dive into.

"It belongs to the 'rents,"
he said, as if they weren't
even there. "They let
me drive it once in a while."

You could have knocked
me over with a feather
and named me Heather,
I was so blown away.

This was so *way*
my day.

"Where in the heck
do your 'rents
get all this money?"
Twig whispered.

"Are they drug dealers
or something illegal?"

I stared at a beagle
on a leash in the street.

Twig was such a geek.

Jake just snickered.

"The only drug they
do is liquor," he said.

Misty and Vince
ignored us, pouring
blood-red wine
into long-stemmed glasses.

"My 'rents are like
big shots in their jobs
at MTV,"
Jake explained.
"They also buy lots of stocks
on Wall Street.
Investment
can't be beat

for getting ahead,
they always say."

"Cool," Twig said.

"Way cool," I said.

But in my head,
I was thinking,
My pops works at a stinking
Mrs. Smith's pie factory
in Banesville, Pennsylvania.
What's Jake going to say
about that?

Then, feeling fat
but happy, I flashed
a gaping grin at Jake, thinking
that I'd savor every minute
of this party favor
lifesaver wild ride:
my once-in-a-
lifetime slide into
euphoria, starting
at the Waldorf-Astoria.

Always Perform Poems in Public When Someone Wants You To

Tavern on the Green
was the most enchanted restaurant
I'd ever seen:
twinkling white lights
and sculptures of ice.
This was no freaking
Mickey D's, KFC,
Dairy Queen,
or Park-N-Eat.

We were seated
in the Crystal Room,
and it shimmered
with chandeliers.

It was magic,
and so tragic
that Twig didn't
know how to act.
She was wacked,
giddy and not
as witty
as she thought.

When they brought
the dish of butter,
it had a cookie-cutter
green insignia
pressed in the
shape of a
leaping deer.

Twig peered
at the logo
and said something
so loco:
"Oh, look here!
A John Deere
tractor picture,
smack-dab
in the middle
of the butter pat!"

Misty batted
her mascara-
brash lashes.

"Twiggy, darling," she said,
"that's the Tavern
on the Green's
trademark:
a leaping deer."

"Don't forget
that these chicks
live in the sticks,"
Jake said with
a wink.

I could have fainted.
Only someone
from Banesville
could have been
so clueless.
Twig could make
a career
out of being weird.

Our waiter—
named Weston—

addressed
our table.

"Ladies," he said
to Twig and me,
"it's refreshing:
a breath of fresh air
to have girls
from the country."

"They're poets,"
said Jake,
as if that
explained us.
"Sister Slam
and Twig."

"Splendid!"
said Weston.
"Impressive."

"Let's have
a recitation
right here,
right now,
in the restaurant,
for the rest of

the customers,"
said Misty.
"I've been here
when they've had
musicians and other
entertainers. Now
it's time for poets."

"Come on," said Vince.
"Just for us."

I was flustered
but mustered
enough guts
to say, "We mostly
do poetry slams."

Weston applauded,
and the white cloth
fell from his arm.

"Charming," he said,
"how darling
farm girls
can become poets!"

"Come on, girls,"
said Vince.
"Show us
how you slam."

I looked at Twig,
and she looked at
me, and I was
weak in the knees.

"You go first,"
I said to Twig.

Twig leaped to
her feet, and
the heat in
her face made
her cheeks flush.

Weston hushed
the customers
in the Crystal Room.

"We have a unique
treat tonight,"
he announced,
bouncing on his heels.

"Two teen poets—
Sister Slam and Twig—
will delight you
as they recite to you."

People clapped,
and Twig rapped
out her poem
about John Lennon
being dead,
leaving Yoko alone
in the bed,
and man,
did her face
turn red
when this
guy named Ted said
that he was
with the *Village Voice*
and liked her choice
of rhymes.

The room exploded
with applause, whistles,
and hurrahs.

It was my turn
to work.
I felt like
a weirdo,
with everybody staring
and the glaring
of a camera's flash
from across the room.

I thought
of doing
my Gloom Pillows
and Huge Boobs poem,
but the mood
in the Crystal Room
was too upbeat
for doom.

I thought
of doing my
Lemon Pie Guy poem,
but thought
of what Twig had said
about how being mean
to people gets you nowhere.

And then I thought
of Mom, and how she believed
in being nice every day
of her way-too-short life.

Dazed, in a haze,
I decided
to recite a poem
that I'd written
trying to get over
Mom's death.

I took a breath
and began:

Another sundown,
low sunken gold.
Nights keep
on going, whole sky's
growing old.
Don't hold on
to busted junk,
dusty love, green lust,
dead sea monkeys . . .
rusty stuff nobody needs.
Throw out the fake pearls.
Bring on the love beads.

At the speed of
a beating heart,
part with the broken,
hoping to start tomorrow
soaking up free borrowed sun.
Old sorrows laid low. A new day's begun.

I was shaking,
raking my hands
through my hair.

"More!" said Jake,
and it thrilled me to the core.

So I did my other poem about Mom,
which starts like this:
All that's left here
is your empty chair.
You're in the air,
and I'm a millionaire
for loving you.

There wasn't
a cough
or a whisper
as Sister
slammed.

You could
have heard
a napkin drop
as I bebopped
and hip-hopped
my way through
the best poems
I ever wrote.

By the time
I finished,
I was shivering
with nerves, and our
meal was served.

I was gliding, wowed,
on Cloud Number Nine,
feeling so fine,
like I was surrounded
by angels. It was strange:
I *actually felt*
something brush
against my face—
like a swishing of
wings or lace—
but nothing was there.

Expect Magic

Hot New Poets in the City:
Sister Slam and Twig
Staying at Waldorf
said the newspaper headline.

I had to admit
that it wasn't a bad picture:
I looked chunky but funky,
and the gap in my teeth
was actually kind of cute.

The article
quoted our poems,
and it said
that our words
were smoking,
and that we
had the Tavern

exploding, titillated
with a tizzy
of electricity.

Jake said
it was a necessity
to get in line for at least
three copies
of the *Village Voice*,
so we did,
and then we cut
out the pictures of us.

Jake taped
one to the outside of
the hotel room door
as his parents snored.

"Poetry galore!" he announced.
"Come explore the candy store
of hard-core poetry like you've
never heard it before!"

We left Jake's 'rents sleeping
and went to eat breakfast at Peacock Alley,
where they had lilies of the valley
and ice-carved hearts on the tables.

"Look," Jake said, tracing the shape
of the ice. "You're melting this heart,
just like you melt mine."

Twig rolled her eyes.
"Oh, brother. Butter her up, why
don't you?"

"You're just jealous," I said,
drizzling syrup on my french toast,
"because Jake likes me the most."

"You don't have to boast," Twig said.

I was a mess:
wearing the same dress
I'd worn yesterday.
Twig was wearing
one of Misty's Liz Claiborne
corny sporty getups,
and she looked ridiculous:
all meticulous like a
country club mother or something.

I still hadn't called Pops,
and Twig wasn't big
on calling her parents either.

We guessed
that Jake's 'rents
had forgotten
all about the calls.

"Enough alcohol,"
Jake said,
"and they can forget
their own address."

We headed back to Floor
Forty-Four, and there
at the door of room Four
Hundred Forty-Four
was a dude with dreadlocks, knocking.

"Yo," said Jake.
"What's up?"

"Zup," said the guy.
"My name's Rafe. I work
at the Nuyorican Poets Cafe.
I'm here to speak to the freaky
Sister Slam and Twig, the chicks in the
news."

"That would be us," said Twig.

"I'm here to invite you
to our slam tonight," said
the man. He moved his hand,
and a little jingle bell
ring tinkled on his finger.

I looked at Twig,
and she looked at me.
"Cool," said Twig.

"Go for it," said Jake.

"Well," I said, "I need to visit
a thrift shop first.
Get some new
threads. If my
hair was long
enough, I'd
even get dreads!"

"Girl," said the dude,
"you're perfect
just as you are:
a rising star
in the slam galaxy."

"Yes," I said.
"We'll be there."

"Don't be square,"
said the guy
with the dreadlocked hair.
"Eight o'clock sharp."

"I'll ride in the cab
with you two," said Jake.
"That way, I'll know
you're safe."

Hearing the
heavenlike
strum of a harp
in my head, I spread
my arms like wings
and began to sing
inside, because
I knew that tonight
would change my life.

Lesson 19

Never Expect a Marshmallow Fluff Kind of Life to Last Forever

That's where it all began:
with the slam that whammed
the boho poetry community.

We started
at the Nuyorican
Poets Cafe,
which was jammed
with people
much cooler than me.

"I am so nervous,"
I whispered to Twig,
fidgeting, jittery,
biting my nails
as we waited to perform.

"Do you have
butterflies in your gut?"
muttered Twig,
chewing on a strand of hair.

"I've got more than
butterflies," I replied.
"I've got flocks of birds
in there."

I was wearing a lavender-purple
furry shirt and a gauze skirt
from a thrift store called Zorro's Digs.

Twig wore camouflage
from the Army/Navy store.

Jake had insisted on paying
for the clothes.
"Your new slam wardrobes!"
he said. "A gift of good luck."

"How do I look?" I asked,
and Jake touched my hand.

"Perfect," he said.
"You're the hottest
chick here."

He cast a glance
at Twig, who wasn't
even listening.

"You and Twig," Jake said.
"You're the two coolest
girls in the room."

Too soon, my name was called,
and Jake looked straight
into my eyes.

"Pretend it's only you
in the room," he said.
"You and your mom.
Just do the poems for her.

"That purple fur
on your shirt," he added,
"makes your eyes
look almost black.
Way attractive."

I almost had a heart
attack when Jake
leaned closer and
pecked my cheek.

"Go slam, Sister," he whispered.

Shaking, I made my
way to the microphone,
combat boots clopping.
Taking a deep breath,
I started to slam.

That's where it all began.

The next night
we went to Jimmy's Uptown.
I wore blue boots and a shimmery
silver prom gown
(from a used-clothes store
called Second Time Around).
Twig dressed in a clown
outfit, and we did slam poems
that made the people laugh.

"Encore! More!" somebody yelled.
It was a girl . . . no, it was a man,

wearing a yellow dress with pearls.
He had long blond hair,
and I stared.

"Girlfriend," he
shouted, "you rock! You're a jammin'
rammer of a slam poet woman!"

It was the Newark Tooth Fairy!
"Yellow is your color," I said
when he came up to the stage
and asked for my autograph.

"It's a small world,"
he said. "Karma brought us
together again."

The Bowery Poetry
Club was next,
and when the judges
held up their cards,
Twig and I had both
scored all 10s.

"Let's get a Mercedes
Benz," Twig joked,
counting the

five-hundred-dollar
cash prize
we'd divide.

A dude named Scarecrow,
with hair of indigo blue,
made our dreams
come true that night
by inviting us to join
him in forming
a new slam team.

"Let's go on the circuit
and work it," he said.

I felt like this
was my birth.

"We need day
jobs, though," said
Twig. "We're running
out of money."

"No prob," said Scarecrow.
"I'll employ both of you
in my shop, The Joy of Soy."

"We'll take it," I said.

Curled on the
sofa in the Waldorf
later that night,
tired but wired,
I was so hyped
that I couldn't sleep.

"Try counting sheep,"
Jake suggested,
and then he made
microwave hot chocolate to
help me relax.

Vince and Misty
were sacked out,
and Twig was actually
slamming in her sleep,
grinding her teeth,
dreaming of poetry.

The moon
was full and gleaming,
its sheen streaming
beams through the
windows of the suite.

"Only two more days
of vacation,"
Jake said.
"It'll suck to go back
to work in Jersey."

"You don't like your job?"
I asked, and he shrugged.

"It's okay," Jake said.
"I just don't know if I
want to spend the rest of
my life in Doozy's Music Store,
helping losers choose amps and
microphone stands."

"So what do you want to do,
for forever?" I asked.

"Make music," Jake said.
"And make money doing it."

"That's cool," I said.
"The number one rule
of life is doing what you like."

I sipped the hot cocoa,
and Jake picked up

his guitar, softly strumming
chords, humming.

"It's bumming me out
to think of you not being
around," I said.

"It's not that far," Jake said,
caressing his guitar.
"I'll come for every weekend slam
that I can. I'm your number one
fan. A Sister Slam groupie!"

I smiled, and filed the
moment in my memory.

"Drive defensively," I said.
"You never know what kind of
maniac's going to smash into you."

Twig and I
started our day jobs
the next morning.

"Is that a Twinkie?" asked Twig,
and I hid the cupcake behind my
back.

"Ssh," I said. "*Twinkie* is a curse
word here in the health food world."

After work, Twig and I entered a frenzied
night world of swirled words,
on the brink of something big.

The gig was packed,
with hackers selling tickets
at hiked prices outside.

By Friday, when it was time
to tell Jake and
his parents good-bye,
Twig and I had made enough money
to rent a miniature persimmon-
walled room with no furniture.

"We need a sofa and a chair,"
said Twig, combing her hair.
Her voice echoed in the empty room.

"No, first we need beds and
food," I said.

"I'd say that your first priority
is a good bolt for the door,"

said Jake. "You've got to be safe."
Jake checked the window, making
sure that it was locked.

It was a full moon.

"See you soon,"
Jake said to Twig, and
we went outside.
Jake intertwined his fingers
with mine, and my skin tingled.

"See you next week," he said,
and he kissed my cheek.

I said okay, and
my head ached as I
watched him walk away.

In the morning, I called Pops
from Scarecrow's shop, filling him in
on everything that had happened in one
short, important week.

"You're not getting
married or anything?"
Pops joked.

"I'm a wide-load
bride," I replied.
"I'm married to poems;
carried across the threshold
of a whole new life!"

"Just be careful,"
Pops said. "The city
is so big."

It was time for the whirlwind
to begin. The gigs were a blur,
a haze of faces and words.
Sometimes, hearing my
own husky voice slicing spicy through
the microphone in a dusky, musky room,
I thought of how nobody would
believe this back home.

With elastic disco clothes and
purple plastic bows, I was spastic.

"We are Sister Slam,
Twig, and the Poetic
Motormouth Road Trip!"
I screamed night after
night, spazzed by success.

I jolted the groupies
with tick-tocking
bolts of shock, kicking
butt when the tickets
sold out and the doors
were locked. It
rocked when a fan-man
named Brock asked
for my socks as a souvenir.

"Here," I said, and I tossed my
stinky socks into the crowd,
where there was a loud scuffle
as three guys tried to grab them.

It was surreal: a crazy-hazy
daisy petal of a heavy metal
dream made real by just
stealing words from
the dictionary and mixing them up.

"We're missionaries,"
Twig said one night.
"We preach the letters of
the alphabet, and how they
can save you, if you
combine them just right."

I stopped having stage fright,
and wore lots of white leather
and feathery boas, with psycho
go-go boots from The BoBo Shop.

"You look hot," Jake said,
on the weekend.

"Not," I said.

"Hot,"
he said. "I should stay
here all week
to protect you from the freaks."

That night,
in the violet
spotlights, a strange shining
knight in silver armor
invited me to a toxic waste site.
"Red spider mites bite
you until you turn blue,"
said Mister Cuckoo.

"No, thank you," I replied.

"But I love you,"
said the man, and it
was the sock fan Brock, screaming
heebie-jeebie-like.
"Jake!" I yelled,
and he came
from backstage
and stood by my side.

"I'm her bodyguard,"
he said. "Protector
of the Sister. Don't
mess with her."

The cops came and shoved Brock
from the club, and Jake looked buff
with his Sister-protecting biceps flexed.

"See," Jake said.
"You need me
to protect you from the freaks."

"Right now," I said, "I need sleep."

"Me too," said Jake. "And my
parents will kill me if I don't
get home."

Twig and I were hip, our lips slicked
watermelon pink and our hair
streaked with the color of
the week. We reeked
of rhyme and wrote poems
all the time. Twig and I also
bickered like sisters over stuff like whose
turn it was to wash the dishes.

"I wish I had my own place," Twig
complained after telling me what
a pain I was. "You're hard to live
with," she said. "Kind of a diva."

I got a slim Creamsicle-colored cell phone
with a ding-a-ling ring, making sure that
the call zone included Jake's home.

On weekdays, I missed Jake like crazy,
and I wrote a boatload of woeful
wicked Jake-sick poems.

We spoke every day
on Jake's lunch break
at Doozy's Music Store.

"What's up?" Jake would say.

"Everything's okay," I'd say.

One day, Jake sounded
blue. "I'm really missing
you," he said.
"You have no clue."

"Oh, yes, I do. I miss you, too."

It was a flurry of busy stuff:
a Marshmallow Fluff cream-puff existence.

But the phone rang late
one starless
September night when
the sky was crying
and black, and it
was Twig's dad, Jack.

"Laura," he said,
out of breath,
"your father had a heart attack."

Always Go Home When There's Trouble

I crumpled
to the floor.
"I can't handle it
if I lose my only
parent," I said out loud.
"There's no way I can
be an orphan. A girl
needs a parent on this
scary planet."

I needed to ditch
this city, quick,
and make my way
to the Banesville Hospital,
but I had no car of my
own. Twig and I
sometimes borrowed

an old gold
Ford, but it was a loan
from Scarecrow.

Home. I want to go home.
I ripped a comb through my hair
and stepped into a pair of sweatpants
and boots. I was still wearing my Misfits
nightshirt.
Home. There's no place like home.
I was Dorothy in *The Wizard
of Oz*, but Sister in the City,
clicking together the heels
of my glittery red Doc Martens.

"Twig," I said, and she sat up,
rumpled and bleary, mascara
smeary, weary from a late-night slam.

"Pops had a heart attack.
I need to go home.
Are you with me,
or are you staying here?"

"I'm with you, come hell
or no hair gel," Twig said.

"But what about
how you jumped out
of the car on the
way here?" I asked.

"Temporary
carsick-chick insanity,"
said Twig. "You know
we're superglued at the hips,
and at the hearts, too."

I tried to smile.

"Should we take a bus
to Banesville?"
Twig suggested.
"Or maybe it'd be best
to take the train."

Shaky, quaking, scared awake,
I called Jake, even though it was late,
to get his advice.

"Sit tight," he said.
"I'll be right there."

Jake must have raced, and his
face was pasty white when
he squealed and peeled
to the curb, then leaped up
the steps six at a time.

"Oh, my God.
You have hives!" he said,
touching my neck.

I was a wreck,
stressed breathless.
"I'm glad you're here,"
I blubbered, then collapsed
into Jake's strong embrace.

He stroked my face.
"It'll be okay.
We'll pray, okay?
No way that it won't be
okay," Jake said.

"Yeah," Twig agreed.
"Pops is strong.
Nothing will go wrong."

"Let's roll," Jake said, taking
control, which was my goal.

We piled into Jake's
car and started
on the far drive home,
leaving the neon
lights and taxi traffic
of the city behind.

In the dismal darkness
of the Lincoln Tunnel,
I blew my nose
on a paper napkin
I'd found on the floor
of Jake's car.
"Thanks for coming
with me, you two," I said.

"We'd be maggots
not to go with you,"
Jake said,
and he reached
over and squeezed
my hand.

"This is what friends
are for: to stick with
you when life sucks," Twig said.

"Life does suck on
occasion," I said.

When I was nine,
and Pops told me
that Mom had died,
I'd thrown myself
on my bed, hopeless and angry,
banging my head
and wishing that I were dead
instead of her. I wore
Mom's flowered nightgown
that night, and about a thousand
nights after,
holding tight to the scent of Mom.

"If Pops dies," I said, "I won't be able
to handle it. It'll kill me.
I can't go through it again."

We each melted
into our seat-belted selves
and rode in eerie silence
until the knifelike
sharp lights of the hospital
whittled holes in the sky,

carving, cutting through darkness,
as I hoped with all my breath
that my pops wasn't dead.

Never Let Doctors Blame You for Their Patients' Problems

It smelled like
Lysol and dying
flesh and wet diapers
in intensive care,
where defenseless
people have to wear
those senseless gowns
that are all open down
the back, exposing
butt cracks and stuff.

It was bad enough
that Pops was in
the hospital,
but seeing him sleeping
in that dress—

pale and helpless—
made me catch
my breath.

It felt like
death, and
hearses, and I
accidentally
cursed at a
nurse clomping
past, chomping
on Starbursts.

"Quiet! Holy
hell! Can't you
tell people are
trying to sleep
in this bleepin'
place?" I raged.
Then I felt like
an imbecile, because
I made more noise
than the nurse.

Pops opened his eyes.

"Laura," he whispered,
his words a wisp.
"Baby. I was going
crazy, waiting."

I cracked, and fritters of Sister Slam
fell in fragments to the hospital bed.

I kissed Pops's
creased cheeks
nineteen times each,
weeping like a freaking idiot.

Pops's face was tinted
ghostly Coast-soap
blue, and I didn't
have a clue
what he was hooked
up to.
An IV, beeping machines,
a tangled
ivylike vine
of wires, and lights
like fires burning were all
connected to Pops.
There was a
lighted road map

of his heart
on a screen.

The room was dim,
and we were lit
by the red lights
of Pop's broken heart.

The old geezer
Doctor Proctor
(known by everybody
in Banesville)
was wearing cruddy green
scrubs with
red blood blotches,
and he was crotchety.

"The surgery went fine,"
he snapped. Then he gave me
a line of crap about how
my father was bothered
by his daughter's AWOL,
and how I ought to be ashamed
and maybe even blamed
for causing all the stress
and distress that might

have made
Pop's heart explode.

"Whoa, dude," said Jake.
"Nobody's to blame.
No offense, sir,
but it's not
Laura's fault."

"No, it's not," said Pops.
"It's not Laura's
fault. It's all the
malted milk shakes
and Tastykakes I ate.
Give Laura a break, Doc."

"Put a sock in it," said
Twig, as Doctor Proctor
stomped off without another word.

Pops grinned. "Hi, Twig,"
he said.

Twig leaned over Pops's
hospital bed and kissed
his bald head.

"They said I'm lucky
to be alive," Pops said.

"I'm lucky, too," I said.
"I don't know what I'd do
without you. Seriously. I'd be
deliriously wacked.
They'd have to lock me
in a padded room."

"It's true," Twig said.
"She'd be a lunatic
without you."

Pops touched my cheek,
and we didn't speak, as
nurses squeaked
by and a baby
began to cry
from somewhere
out there.

"So how was your
poetry tour?"
Pops asked,
and I grinned.

"Cool," I answered.
"It's too hard to
make a
long story
short. I'll try to
explain it
later. By
the way,
this is Jake.
He saved
my life."

Pops was a
gentleman,
even in a
dress, and
he shook
Jake's hand.

"Pleased to meet
you, Jake," he said.
"Thanks for
looking out for my
baby girl.
She's the
only one
I've got."

"No problem,"
said Jake.

"He's my
best friend,"
I said, but then
Twig glared.

"After Twig,"
I said.

Pops rubbed
his head, a
faraway gaze
in his faded
blue eyes. "When
the pain in my chest
started," he said,
"I had a vision
of you two—
Twig and Laura—
and you were
big stars, driving
fancy cars and
signing autographs.
Then I saw Mom,
right before everything

went black
with the heart attack."

"Wow," I said,
and took a big
breath. "Pow."

I sat down
on the edge of
Pops's bed.

"So how's
Mrs. Smith's
been?" I asked.

"Same old
game," Pops said.
"Cherry pies
churning out
like flies."

"Pops works
in a pie factory,"
I explained to Jake,
no longer ashamed.

"A pie factory," Jake said.
"Cool. Free pies."

Pops's eyes gleamed,
and he seemed to
really be liking Jake.

"What's the meaning of
the Chinese blue tattoo?"
Pops asked.

Jake smiled
and held his
arm to the light.

"Dream, Believe,
Fly," Jake said,
and then we
all got quiet
and watched
the light of Pops's
beating heart.

Lesson 22

Never Take Your Friggin'
Soul Mate for Granted

I was back
in the House
of Crapper,
and I was
happier than ever,
back in the 'hood.
It felt good—
like home,
only better.
Pops never said
one word about me
wrecking the Firebird,
and he laminated and framed
the news photos of me and
Twig, hanging them all
over the walls.

Back in my toad-colored,
gloom-pillowed room,
with my waterbed
and lava lamp bubbling
water-red, I felt content.

Pops—my 'rent—
was recovering,
and I was hovering:
fluffing his pillows
and dispensing his pills
lined up on
the windowsill.
I was filled
with gratitude,
and my latitude
and attitude
were cool with Pops.

"It's wonderful
to have your music
blaring from the bedroom,"
he said. "I'm so glad to have
you back home."

I got a job
at Bibliophile
Bob's Books,
the only bookstore
for miles,
where the floor
had black and purple tiles,
and the ceiling was painted
with strange deranged angels
playing electric guitars
instead of harps.

"Aren't you Laura Crapper?"
asked the customers, and
I got looks of respect
mixed with envy
because they'd
seen the headlines
in the local paper
about my poetry caper.

"A.K.A. Sister Slam,"
I replied.

Twig was working
at Wild Child's
Beef Jerky,

and we called Scarecrow
to tell him that
we were back home.

"You're letting your
apartment go?" he asked.
"Bummer."

"It was a good summer,"
I said. "But Pops needs me."

Jake and I talked every
day—about everything from
temporary hair dyes
to lemon pies. We
dragged out our good-byes,
and Jake said that I
was his light on moonless
nights, like he was mine.

"You two make me sick," Twig
complained. "You're like a crack
addict, except that you're
addicted to Jake."

"You're just jealous," I responded,
"because your brand-new boyfriend, *Ron*,

drives a rattletrap *Honda*
and isn't nearly as hot as Jake."

On Halloween,
his face painted
lizard-green,
Jake came and we
went trick or treating,
with me teetering in glittery
red *Wizard of Oz*
shoes. Twig's costume
was a floozy, and her
doozy of a boyfriend
didn't even need a mask.

Thumbing our noses
at the ridiculous Banesville
rule about not being
over thirteen for trick
or treat, we walked
door-to-door, collecting candy
in pumpkin buckets.

"Let's see how many
treats we can eat before
midnight," Jake
said, and Twig,

thinner than ever,
was the big winner
of a miniature
candy-bar dinner.

In November,
I drove Pops's
Chevy, alone,
(Pops was too tired to go,
he said) to Jersey
and had Thanksgiving dinner
in an expensive restaurant
with Misty and Vince
and Jake.

"Everybody say
what you're grateful for,"
said Misty,
and we listed gratitudes.

Mine included
Pops, my job, Twig,
and of course Jake.

"I'm grateful for Laura,
my car, and my guitar," said
Jake. "In that order."

Late that night, I hated
to leave Jake waving
in the rearview mirror.

"Peace out!"
he shouted. "Ciao!
Keep your eyes
on the road."

I blew him
an invisible kiss,
then drove
home thinking
about how
Jake's eyes
caught the star glow.

He called
as soon as I
got back home.

"Just wanted
to say that I
really meant
what I said,"
he said.

"What: Peace out?"
I asked. "Ciao?
Keep my eyes on
the road?"

"No, crazy," Jake said.
"About being
grateful for you,
the car, and the guitar,
in that order.
No girl's ever had
that honor before."

"Well, this is one
flattered fat chick," I said.

"Laura," said Jake,
"please don't say stuff
like that. Don't call
yourself fat. You are
the coolest girl I know."

But then,
in the beginning
of the freezing
winter season,
for no reason

that I knew,
from out of
the cold blue on December
twenty-two,
Jake's calls stopped,
and my pillows
were sopped
from sobbing.

"I'm wrecked,
a mess, in distress,
feeling less
alive than
dead," I said
to Twig.

"It's not even been a week,"
she said. "Maybe he has
laryngitis and can't speak."

I tried to
be cool,
but I felt
like such
a fool.

"There are
lots more sharks
in the aquarium,"
Twig said.
"We'll go to
the Guy-arium
and buy one
on sale.
Dudes are
a dime
a dozen."

"Maybe he
found some
hussy," I fussed.

"So bust him. Call.
E-mail. Drive to Jersey."

I shook my head.

"I don't want to
seem desperate,
even though I am," I said.

"Forget him," said
Twig. "He's only

one of a trillion
male species beasts."

"But Twig,
Jake is my friggin'
soul mate.
I'm wiggin' out without
him, not diggin'
it big time."

"Get a grip,"
said Twig.
"It's been only
three freakin'
days, Laura."

"But I hate
days without
Jake," I said. "It's
like German
chocolate cake
without the icing.
Like blades
slicing my
heart, or
Cupid shooting
poison-ass darts,

or somebody
stealing my
Pop Tarts.
Life farts without
Jake in it."

"Ohmygod. It's been only
three days," Twig repeated.

"But three days
without Jake is like
a year without anybody
else," I muttered,
and Twig shuddered.

"It's not like he's water
or air," she said.
"You don't need him to survive.
You can stay alive
without a drink of Jake."

Twig grinned.
"Hey, I just had a brainstorm!
How about I fix you up
with that divorced guy Norm,
from my work?"

"He's a jerk," I said.
"I don't want some
beef jerky dude.
Not to be rude,
Twig, but no thanks."

"Listen, Sister," Twig said.
"You're a girl who doesn't
need pearls or curls or
a romance with a man. You can
stand on your own two
combat-boot feet."

I was bummed,
and my cup
was empty. I
was a Humpty
Dumpty fallen
off the wall.
I tried to call
again and again
but just kept getting
the beeps of the machine.

There was a
blue hole in my soul.

I coped with a poem:
I've paid the debt
of deep regret.
Lamented, repented,
yet stuck in cement.
I can smoke another cigarette,
get myself a red Corvette,
eat another crepe suzette,
drink lots of anisette.
But there's one thing
I can't forget:
the shadow of his silhouette.

"Get a grip," Twig said.
"You don't smoke
or drink."

"I think that I might
start," I said.
Then I went
to bed, feeling dead
in my head,
and in my legs,
and most definitely
in the red of my heart.

Dream, Believe, Fly

It was Christmas Eve,
and our holiday doorbell
chimed to the tune of
"Silent Night."

"We have too much
annoying joyful noise
in this house," I groused to Pops.

Pops is into all this animated
Christmas stuff: Santa snoring,
Mrs. Claus pouring milk,
motion-activated elves putting
toys on shelves.

Pops and I had
cookies galore
from the

Wal-Mart store,
but still, I felt
bored, out of
sorts, numb to
the core.

"It's Christmas, Sister!"
Pops said, trying to
cheer me by using my slam name.

"Big deal," I said.
"It's just another day."

So anyway,
the doorbell
was blaring away,
and I didn't care
who was there,
because it wasn't
Jake, and Santa
Claus is a fake. I
was a Scrooge, a
grouch with an ouch
in the part of me
that used to believe.

I flung open
the door, and it
was Twig, all
decked out in
this retro
fur coat from
a vintage shop,
with jingle bell
earrings swinging.

She was bringing
my gift, which
was wrapped in
an old road map.

"Hey, Sister,"
she said, and
slapped me a
high five.
"Look alive!
Happy holidays!"

"Yeah," I said.

I was trying to
get into the spirit
of things, wearing

my Rudolph fuzz slippers
and Santa Claus PJs
of red velour.

Twig handed
me the road-
map-wrapped
box. I'd already
given her toe socks
and Pop Rocks
and a clock
that glows pink
in the dark.

"Hark, the herald
Twig does bring!" Twig
said. "Open it!"

I did, and there
was a matching
fur coat, exactly
like Twig's, except
bigger, and a pair
of dingly jingle bell earrings.

"For our next slam,"
Twig said. "Gotta

look good for when
we find another poetry jam."

"I'm jonesing for a
poetry slam," I said.

"You're jonesing for
a certain green-eyed man," Twig said.

I put the earrings in my
lowest hole. I tried
on the coat.

"You look way great,"
Twig pronounced.
"Date bait."

"Yeah," I said.
"Great."

"Somebody just
pulled into the
driveway," Pops
said. "Bet it's
Fred." That was
Pops's bud, a dud
of an old fud.

"Dude!" said Twig,
peering through
the window.
"It's a white limousine!"

It was Jake,
and I freaked.

I hopped
up and down,
looking like a
clown, and
Pops laughed.

"You're half
crazy for that
boy," he said,
and I didn't
deny it.

We watched
as Jake parked
the car, lit by
the stars of
Christmas.

This was
a miracle,
the pinnacle,
and I was *so*
not cynical.

"Joy to the world,"
I belted out,
"the dude has come!"

"Don't act so dumb," Pops said.
"He'll think you're one fry
short of a Happy Meal."

I squealed, and then
got myself together
before I ventured outside.

"Hey, Jake," I said,
calm as milk, smooth
as silk in my Santa
PJs and white fur coat.

Jake smiled
and threw his
arms wide, and

I couldn't hide
my insanity any longer.

I threw myself
at him, and Jake
hugged me tight
in the snow-flurry night.

"I have a surprise,"
Jake whispered.

I shivered,
and he lifted his guitar
from the car.

We went into
the living room,
where our aluminum
tree gleamed
silver and green.

Jake beamed
in the sheen
from the tree.

"Sorry that I
haven't called,"

he said, and my
head waltzed
with my heart.
"I've been really busy
working on your gift,
and I just knew that
I'd blow it and spill the secret
if I talked to you."

He started to hum,
then strummed a riff
of chords, his
fingers flashing magic
of wonder and wings
across the strings
of his guitar.

My heart was pinging.
Jake started singing
my poems, the
words of my slams,
turned into
cool, beautiful
tunes, music of
red and yellow
and purple and blue.

"I worked on them
for weeks," Jake said
at the end. "And one
more thing."

He pulled from his pocket
a rockin' silver ring.

"Look inside the
band, the part
that's against
your hand," he said.

Inscribed inside
were etched words:
"Dream, Believe, Fly."

"Well, try
it on!" Jake said,
and I did. It fit
perfectly.

"Your present," I blubbered,
"is a whole bunch of
poems. I'll read them
to you later, when I

can talk. I also got
you some awesome
guitar picks."

"Cool," said Jake.
"And there's one
more thing, from
my 'rents, for Twig
and you: a gig on
the Starlight Roof
of the Waldorf-
Astoria. You'll
slam some, and then
I'll play the songs
with your words.
Not promising
anything, but
Mom and Dad
did this rad
thing: they
arranged for
the MTV people
to be there.
You know:
people on the
go, people in
the know,

people who
make shows.
Who knows:
maybe a video
will end up
on MTV!"

"Sweet!" I shrieked,
and Twig freaked.
She screamed.

"What about Ron?" I asked,
and she waved her hand.

"Ron who? He'll find something
else to do."

"Pops is coming, too,
to see you two
do your thing,"
Jake said. "We're
leaving tonight.
The 'rents are paying
for a week at the
Waldorf, so we'll
all be there for
New Year's Eve."

"I can't believe
this!" I squeaked. "Sweet!"

Jake lifted
his guitar.
"I called Scarecrow
to let him know.
Ready to go?"

"No," I said.
"Not yet.
There's something
I need to do
first. Something
that Pops and I
haven't done
for way too long.
It was once
a tradition
on Christmas Eve,
but we just couldn't seem
to keep it up
after Mom died."

Twig smiled.
She read my mind.

"It's time
to start the tradition
again," she said.

I went to my bedroom,
and there on the shelf
were all of the
books we'd read when
I was a kid.

I chose four:
one each for Jake
and Twig and Pops
and me.

I read *Green Eggs
and Ham*,
in the style of slam,
and then
Jake read
Frosty the Snowman.
Twig's book was
*The Last Chimney
of Christmas Eve,*
and I could feel
I was starting to

believe in magic
once more.

Then it was Pops's
turn, and the words
of *The Cat in the Hat*
took me back
to Christmas Eve
with Mom.

It was the bomb,
because I felt
Mom's presence,
her essence,
and that was
the best present ever.

"Now we can go,"
I said, and we unplugged
stuff and packed bags.

I remembered Pops's medicine.
"One pill, two pills,
red pill, blue pill," I said,
and then we left the house in
complete darkness,

heading together to
the car.

The stars
in the sky
were at the height
of bright,
and the light
from the moon
lit up the blue
magnetic sign
on the driver's
side door:

SISTER SLAM, TWIG,
AND THE POETIC MOTORMOUTH
ROAD TRIP

I wrapped my arms
around Jake's
neck, and then
we kissed. It
was bliss, kismet,
a blitz of our lips zipped
together, close and warm
and just as I'd
always dreamed

it would be
in the best
serendipity fantasy.

Pops whistled. "Where's
the mistletoe?" he asked.

"Get a room,
you two!" said
Twig, and we
pulled apart,
my heart
doing cartwheels.

Bells were pealing
somewhere in
Banesville, and
flurries of snow
were falling soft
on our noses,
and all of a sudden
there was the smell
of roses.

I breathed in deep.

"What's that smell?"
asked Jake.

"Evergreen," Twig said.
"It's Christmas Eve."

Then, leaving home
behind, we climbed
into the limousine,
and the full moon beamed
a wreath of green-cheese teeth
with a sheath of stars.

We settled into the car
and started our most-hip
road trip—Sister Slam and
Jake, Pops and Twig,
below the moon that lit
both New York City
and home.